OLIVER'S WARS

Also by Budge Wilson

The Worst Christmas Present Ever

Mr. John Bertrand Nijinsky and Charlie

A House Far from Home

Mystery Lights at Blue Harbour

Breakdown

Thirteen Never Changes

Going Bananas

Madame Belzile and Ramsay Hitherton-Hobbs

The Leaving

Lorinda's Diary

BUDGE WILSON
OLIVER'S WARS

For Taylor —
Keep writing!
Nice to meet you.

Budge Wilson

Stoddart

A JUNIOR GEMINI BOOK

Published in 1994 by
Stoddart Publishing Co. Limited
34 Lesmill Road
Toronto, Canada
M3B 2T6
(416) 445-3333

Second printing August 1994

First published as an Irwin Junior Fiction Book
in 1992 by
Stoddart Publishing Co. Limited

Canadian Cataloguing in Publication Data

Wilson, Budge
Oliver's wars

Junior Gemini ed.
ISBN 0-7736-7416-0

I. Title

PS8595.I5805 1994   jC813'.54   C94-930126-4
PZ7.W5505 1994

Cover Design: Brant Cowie/ArtPlus Ltd.
Cover Illustration: David Craig
Typesetting: Tony Gordon Ltd.

Printed and bound in the United States of America

*Stoddart Publishing gratefully acknowledges the support of the
Canada Council, the Ontario Ministry of Culture, Tourism, and
Recreation, Ontario Arts Council, and Ontario Publishing Centre
in the development of writing and publishing in Canada.*

This book
is for
Captain Harold Jarche

Acknowledgments

I would like to thank the following:

The Department of Tourism and Culture of the Province of Nova Scotia for a Grant in Aid to Established Writers to assist me while writing *Oliver's Wars*.

Captain Harold Jarche of 313 Field Hospital, Lahr, Germany, and Warrant Officer David Peltier, Base Hospital, CFB Moose Jaw, for providing me with useful military and medical information.

The students and staff of Tower Road School, who have kindly permitted me a few inaccuracies.

Lotte Springer, in whose house I wrote this book.

Sheila Dalton.

And Alan Wilson.

One

Oliver Kovak looked out the plane window and tried to concentrate on the bank of clouds below him. Beside him sat his twin brother, Jerry, twiddling his thumbs and restlessly crossing and uncrossing his legs. It wouldn't be Jerry's turn for the window seat for twenty more minutes. Oliver sat quietly, with his hands clasped together in his lap. But if you looked carefully, you would have seen that his knuckles were white and that his eyebrows were drawn together in a frown. He was thinking, and most of his thoughts were troubling ones.

In the seat behind Oliver and Jerry sat their mother. Her eyes were on a magazine she was holding, but she wasn't really reading it. Like Oliver, she was thinking, and her frown was even deeper than his. It was a long journey from Moose Jaw to Halifax, but she was too tired to feel either restless or bored. Besides, her thoughts were keeping her so busy that she had no energy left for anything else. Not just then, anyway.

Mrs. Kovak sighed, and stroked her forehead with her middle finger. A headache was coming on. That's all she needed at the moment. She looked around the seat at Oliver and Jerry. Jerry was fidgeting as usual; it was always hard for him to sit still for long. And there was Oliver, so still and quiet. Mrs. Kovak wished she could be like him. Nothing ever seemed to bother Oliver. He looked at the world with such a steady, peaceful gaze. Just like his father. She sighed again.

Oliver looked up and saw the flight attendant approaching with a tray of drinks and cookies. "A Pepsi," he mumbled when she asked what he wanted; then he took it from her, forgetting to say thank-you. Jerry didn't even ask for anything. Oliver had to nudge him to get his attention. He was slumped down beside his brother, frowning, staring at the seat ahead of him, chewing on his thumbnail and kicking his hand luggage.

Oliver couldn't ever remember a two-week period as awful as the one they'd all just lived through. It was hard to believe it had only been fourteen days long. First there had been the message to his father at the military base, telling him he would have to join the hospital unit in the Persian Gulf.

Oliver would never forget where he had been or what he'd been doing on the afternoon he'd heard that news. He was working on a jigsaw puzzle in the living room — a big one with a thousand pieces. The family always had one set up during December and early January, because people were at home more often and could work on it off and on during the holidays.

The puzzle picture was of a tray of candies — chocolates, jellybeans, and gumdrops. When his father told him he was going to have to go to the Gulf, Oliver just sat there and stared at all those dumb pieces. He couldn't even look at his father. His eyes were fixed on the part of the puzzle that was done — the brown shiny chocolates and the candies wrapped in gold and silver paper. He wanted to grab the whole cloth and pull it off the table, scattering all the pieces from one end of the room to the other. He wanted to pick up his mother's favorite brass candlestick and throw it clear through the picture window.

But he didn't do any of those things. He just sat and glared at the puzzle. He hadn't been able to eat a candy or a chocolate since that day. Later on, he heard his father say, "He took it really well. He didn't even cry."

Everyone reacted differently to the news. Jerry was scared. His eyes sort of bugged out of his head, and he yelled at his father, "You *can't* leave us and go way over there and get killed! Who'll look after us?" Then he'd stamped around, slamming doors and hitting things. But that hadn't lasted for long. Soon he tore out of the house and rushed off to tell his pals that his father was going to be in the war. He seemed almost . . . *pleased*.

But his mother — *she* knew what a war *was*. Her own father and mother had been kids in Halifax during World War II, and they'd told her many scary stories about what life had been like back then. When her husband told her his news, she didn't cry or anything. Not right then, anyway. But her eyes had opened so wide — a little bit like Jerry's — that they looked almost round; and they had, oh, such a wild and terrified look in them. Oliver saw it when he finally looked up from his puzzle. His mother flew into his father's arms, and dug her fingernails into his shoulders, making awful groaning noises. Then she stepped back and cried out to him:

"Why do they need *you*? Oh, I know you're in the army and I know you're a nurse, but there are hundreds of nurses in the services. Young girls. Why don't they use *them*? They're single and they're free — most of them anyway. They'd probably even like the adventure. But you're a family man, Sam. You've got *two kids*. How can they do this to us?"

Oliver's father took both her hands in his, and looked so sad and . . . *sorry*. In fact, he even said he was. "I'm sorry, Jill," he'd said. "But they need male nurses extra badly. Most of the casualties will be men — big ones and heavy ones. They need people strong enough to turn them and lift them, and to move heavy equipment." Then he'd hugged her some more.

Jerry had the window seat now, so Oliver just stared into space. He thought about the fathers of some of his friends. Some of them were okay, but many of them were often cross and impatient, forever pushing their kids to get high marks and win races and things.

Then he thought about his own father. As he did, he felt the tension come out of his knuckles, and the tight spot between his eyebrows loosen up. Such a great guy. So fair, and almost always good-natured and easy to get along with. *Happy*. Yes, that was the right word. He seemed to be a really happy man. Oliver let his mind slide over some of the fun times he'd had with his dad — cross-country skiing, reading books together, shopping with him for birthday presents for his mother, watching the Cosby show with him each evening. When he wasn't working at the hospital, the thing his dad seemed to want most of all was just to be with his family. He was stern sometimes, but never mean or mad.

And now he was gone. He was somewhere — in the desert, maybe — bandaging people up and lifting them out of beds, and probably listening to the bombs and guns, and wishing he were back home. Oliver could feel his eyes filling with tears again. He turned his face to the aisle so that Jerry wouldn't see. His mom and dad had said it was okay to cry about the war, but he was too locked up inside himself to do it very often.

As for Jerry, he seemed so tough and angry, and didn't go in for crying. He probably thought he was too big to cry: he was tall and full of muscles, even at twelve. Oliver was lanky, like his father, but short, like his mother. People often said that it would be hard to find a pair of twins so different from one another.

And now they were on their way to a whole new life — for as long as the war would last. They'd figured it might be a long time, so they'd rented out their house in Moose Jaw. After two weeks of decisions and packing and saying good-bye, they were finally on this plane, heading east to a place that Oliver had never seen. By evening, they'd be in Halifax, Nova Scotia — far, far away from the prairies he loved so much.

It was hard to think of living in a place that wasn't flat, that didn't have all that wonderful sky. He thought he'd feel smothered and hemmed in by all the hills in Nova Scotia. He'd heard, too, that they weren't even real mountains, like the Rockies. Just *hills*. Nothing you could get very excited about.

And what would it be like living with other people? He started to rub his thumb and index finger together, making little circular motions, first one way, then the other. He ran his hand through his dark unruly hair, and sighed. Although the other people were his grandparents — his mother's parents — the only times he'd seen them were when they'd visited Moose Jaw — at *his* house and only for a week, every few years. So he really didn't know them.

Oliver wished the family hadn't had to change *everything* in their life right now. It was bad enough to be losing their father, without losing their friends, their school, even their house. But their mother had said that it was necessary. When she'd said it, she'd looked as though she'd been announcing a catastrophe. And as far as Oliver was concerned, that's exactly what she *had* been doing.

She'd tried to explain it all, of course. It would be rough on her to keep a big house running without their father there to help out and do repairs. Also, she was a red-hot computer lady who wanted and needed a job. The company she'd been working for in Saskatchewan had gone bankrupt in December. And now, thanks to a friend of the family, there was a good job waiting for her in Halifax. She couldn't turn it down.

So, here they were, on their way to heaven knew what. Jerry had now had his half-hour by the window, and it was Oliver's turn again. He looked out and saw that the cloud cover had disappeared. Down below was an endless stretch of forest, dotted with small lakes. Where were the fields? Or the houses? Or the roads? What kind of place were they coming to, anyway? He felt a thrill of fear pass through him.

Oliver shut his eyes and leaned back in the seat. I'd like it if just one single solitary thing looked familiar, he thought. He chuckled in a low, sad kind of way. They all think I'm the calm one, the steady one, he mused. A lot they know! They haven't got the foggiest idea what's going on in the inside of my head.

"Fasten your seat belts," said the voice on the loudspeaker. "And stow your hand luggage under the seat in front of you. We're just starting the descent to Halifax International Airport."

Two

After the plane's long descent, traffic problems at the airport prevented it from landing. So it flew in ever-widening circles around the terminal and over the surrounding countryside.

Oliver could see by now that there were houses after all — lots of them — a blanket of houses in Halifax, a city that seemed to spring, like a surprise, right out of the forest. In fact, it *was* a surprise. Oliver found it hard to believe that you could travel from nothing to something so suddenly.

"Hey, look!" he cried to Jerry, poking him in the ribs. There was the sea — beyond the city and around it. He could see that Halifax was shaped like a giant mushroom, with the stem connecting it to the rest of the province. Across the long, wide harbor, joined by two graceful bridges, was the city of Dartmouth: more houses, but also lots of lakes. And on the other side of Halifax was the long stretch of water called the North West Arm.

"Ever neat!" breathed Oliver. "All that water! And look!" He dug Jerry in the ribs again. "Look at that ocean! It just goes on and on. There doesn't seem to be any end to it." Even from this height, he could see that if you were standing in the right place, there might be almost as much sky in Nova Scotia as in Saskatchewan. If you looked out to sea and there was no land in front of your eyes, he figured there'd just *have* to be a lot of sky.

But Jerry just sniffed, and blew something through his nose that sounded like *hmpf*. "Still too many trees," he complained, "and the houses look stupid. Look at them! They're like toy houses. Silly little square things, and colored all sorts of wild colors. I sure hope Grandpa and Grandma live in a half-decent brick bungalow. Or one with white siding. A *normal* house."

"They don't." Their mother had been eavesdropping around the edge of the seat. "Their house is tall and it's blue, so you'd better get used to it. I grew up in it, and I *like* that house."

The twins didn't say anything. What could you say about a blue house that you'd never even seen? Blue! Besides, the plane was returning now to the airport area, and they were flying over dense woods again. The trees and roads were getting bigger and bigger, until suddenly the plane touched the ground with a sharp thud, and raced down the runway with its brakes on and the wing flaps open. Their journey was over.

But the *day* wasn't over. The four of them straggled along the upper level of the terminal ("Like Brown's cows," said their mother) towards the escalator. Down the escalator they went to the main floor, and suddenly found themselves in a large room full of people. Hundreds of eyes were focused on the door, searching for friends and relatives.

And there they were — Mr. and Mrs. Fraser, his grandparents — almost in the front row. Oliver watched as Jerry and his mother rushed forward to be hugged, and heard them all say the things that people say at airports: "So wonderful to see you. . . . How was the flight? . . .

My, how you've grown! . . . Lovely to be here." But all through the greetings, Oliver could see that the only one who really looked pleased was his grandmother.

The five of them moved over to wait for the Kovaks' luggage to come around on the carousel. There seemed to be a lot of cheerful people around, hugging, kissing, laughing — not because anything was funny, but just because they felt so happy. Watching all that joyfulness made Oliver feel even more miserable.

What would happen, he wondered, if people said what they really felt? He thought about what he might say: "I hate being here . . . I miss my friends already . . . You two look too old to be much fun to live with . . . The sea looks okay, but there are too darn many trees." If I said those things, they'd probably turn me right around and send me back on the next plane. He chuckled to himself about this, and when his grandparents first spoke to him, he was smiling.

"Well, *he* looks cheerful," said his grandfather. "I'm glad *someone* is!"

His mother looked terrible, but she gave a short laugh.

"Oh — *him*. Oliver. He's fine. He's *always* fine. Nothing ever bothers him. It would take more than a silly old war to get *him* churned up."

Oliver kept the smile glued to his face, and let his grandmother hug him and his grandfather shake his hand. Why can't he hug me too? wondered Oliver. Why, he asked himself for the hundredth time, is my own father almost the only father I know who hugs his sons? Is there something *wrong* with men hugging people?

"Quiet, though," said Grandma.

"Yes," said his mother. "Very. He's *thinking* all the time."

"Hope he's got something better to do than *that*," retorted Grandpa. "Lots of chores waiting to be done."

Mrs. Kovak sighed, and her voice sounded thin and strained. "He'll *do* them, Dad. Give him a break. *Someone* has to do the thinking. Besides, we're still in the airport. We just *arrived*. We don't need to start doing chores *yet*, do we?"

"Touchy, touchy," said Grandpa. "Haven't changed a bit."

"And you, neither," mumbled Oliver's mother. But her father was a bit deaf, and didn't hear her. However, Oliver did.

* * *

The drive home was surprisingly long, and it was exactly as Oliver thought it would be. Trees as far as you could see — Christmas trees, mostly. Almost no houses, and no fields or farms. Although it was January, there was only a thin dusting of snow on the ground, and the lakes looked as smooth and as perfect as sheets of glass. He watched an iceboat racing up one of the lakes. On another, a group of kids were playing tag on the ice.

Then, all of a sudden, the city just sort of jumped out of the forest, and they were driving down a long ramp into Halifax, with colored box-like houses on all sides and stretching into the distance.

"Weird!" exclaimed Jerry.

Oliver could see his grandfather's neck stiffen. "And what's so weird, may I inquire?" he asked, voice cold.

"All those dinky houses. Everything made of wood. All those crazy colors."

"If you can't say anything nice, Gerald," said Grandpa, "you could at least try to say nothing at all. Moose Jaw doesn't happen to be the only city in the entire world. Besides, you're a guest. Whatever else guests are supposed to be, they're expected to be polite. You could try remembering that, young man."

"Horace," said Grandma, her voice weary. "Please. He's probably tired. It's a long trip. And he's only a child." But she didn't put much ginger into her words, and her husband ignored them. But he drove the rest of the way in a tense silence.

Oliver looked out the window of the car, trying not to listen to that silence. They drove past two big shopping centers, and then down a long winding street between tall trees and big houses. But even those houses were made of wood and were painted many different colors. This wasn't like any other town he'd ever been in. They drove on and on, past what looked like two universities, and into a section of high old houses.

"And here," Grandpa was saying, turning the car into a narrow driveway on the far side of Halifax, "is our own weird house. Made of wood. And blue. I hope you'll be able to endure living in such a peculiar and colorful dwelling." His voice was scornful and cross.

Jerry looked as though he might explode, as though he might take his piece of hand luggage and throw it at his grandfather's head.

"Mother!" whispered Mrs. Kovak, when her father left the car. "Why can't you make him stop? You've been letting him push us around ever since I can remember."

Grandma sighed, and looked sort of . . . what exactly did she look like? wondered Oliver. Well, he thought he knew the answer to that question. She looked *defeated*. But she tried to stand up for herself.

"It's not that simple," she said. "Surely you must know that. There were always lots of battles in this family, and in battles, people certainly get wounded and suffer a lot. But I always figured that if we all stood up to him and fought back too much, we'd have a full-fledged war on our hands — day after awful day. And I didn't think I could stand that." She sighed again.

War. There was that word again. And others. Defeat. Battle. Suffering. Terrible words. Oliver slipped his hand into his mother's, and she squeezed it. He had a strange feeling that he was comforting her, instead of the other way around.

Jerry was kicking the front seat of the car and swearing under his breath. Grandpa was shouting something at them from the front door, and his wife was calling back, "We're coming, dear, we're coming!" Then she turned to Mrs. Kovak and said, "Hurry, darling. Don't keep him waiting. He hates it so when we're slow."

The sad little parade approached the house, and Oliver looked up at it. It was tall and narrow, with two stories plus what he thought must be an attic. It was stuck onto another house that was exactly the same, and it had a flat front with high narrow windows. There was gingerbread carving around the roof and the windows and on the small veranda. It was all made of wood. And it was very blue. Jerry was right. It *was* weird.

In the doorway stood Grandpa, frowning and tapping his foot in impatience. "Get a move on!" he was yelling. "I can't hold this door open all day. You're letting the heat escape!"

Oliver felt the knot in his stomach tighten. "Welcome to Halifax," he whispered.

Three

Afterwards, it was hard for Oliver to remember that first afternoon and evening in Halifax. There were just too many things happening and too much to see. But some things did stand out in his memory: for instance, how skinny the house was, and how tall the ceilings, with all sorts of fancified carving in the plaster surrounding the light fixtures. The stairway seemed to be almost as steep as a ladder, and it led to a narrow hall with three bedrooms off it.

Then the same stairway continued on up to a chilly top floor, where there were a lot of boxes and trunks and discarded junk. Interesting junk. There were old dolls (his mother's?), and some metal toy trucks that must have belonged to Mom's brother. There was a broken-down dressmaking form that looked like a real headless and limbless person, and an ancient treadle sewing machine. There were cartons and cartons of mildewed books and magazines, and packages of letters tied up with faded pink ribbons.

Even on that first day, Oliver wondered about those letters. Who'd written them? Who'd received them? Could they be *love letters* — maybe belonging to his grandparents? His mind had a hard time curling itself around that thought. It was unreal enough to think of his grandfather *saying* something loving and tender, without trying to imagine him writing it all down.

Oliver liked the attic. He even liked the wispy cobwebs and the small friendly spider on the window sill. He had a feeling that somehow or other, this was going to be *his place*.

Coming down the stairs with Jerry, he stroked the shiny wooden bannister. It looked inviting. Maybe sometime when no one was home . . . But Jerry couldn't wait. He climbed up on it, and then let himself hurtle down to the next floor.

"Gerald! *Gerald*!" Grandpa's voice was loud and harsh in the narrow hall. "That's the first and last time I expect to see you do that, my boy. Do you think I want those mahogany railings all scratched up by your shoes? Or to have to write and tell your father that you broke your neck? Get *off*! Jill!" he yelled at their mother. "Do something about that boy!"

Jerry was clinging to the bannister as though it were his only friend. Slowly, he got off and gave his grandfather a fierce dark look before he slunk back up the stairs to his room. Oliver felt a stab of envy. Why couldn't he be like Jerry — flying fearlessly down the bannister in someone else's house and then looking daggers at his grandfather when he was told to stop? Oliver knew he'd never have that kind of courage, not if he lived to be a hundred years old.

Oliver realized that Grandpa *owned* the bannister, and that he had the right to decide whether or not anyone should slide down it. But why couldn't he have waited until tomorrow before he started all that scolding and ordering around? It was going to be hard enough getting used to living in this strange building and peculiar city without being shot down in flames on the very first afternoon. But only Jerry had the courage to show how he felt. Or was it courage? Oliver didn't know.

Supper was baked beans done in a big brown crock, with juicy hunks of squishy salt pork floating around in the bubbling juices. Coleslaw. And hot steamy home-made brown bread. "Your favorite," said Grandma to Oliver's mother. "Besides, it's Saturday night, and lots of us still have beans for supper once a week. Just like the old days, when I was a kid."

Oliver thought about this, later. He couldn't imagine his grandmother as a kid, but oddly, he could easily think of his grandfather as a young boy. Scrappy, I bet, thought Oliver. Getting into fights over every little thing, and mad at anyone and everyone that got in his way. And probably brave — or reckless (whichever was the right word) — skating on thin ice, swimming in water that was way over his head, walking tight-rope-style over rickety broken bridges. And his anger always near the surface, ready to break out at anything or anybody that slowed him up or tried to change his route.

Oliver frowned. Why could he imagine so well what his grandfather might have been like when he was young? And why was he feeling this grudging admira-tion? And then suddenly he knew the answers. It was because his grandfather reminded him of Jerry. Wow! Was that what Jerry was going to be like when he grew up? Oliver grinned. Better warn his brother's future wife about what she might be getting into.

"Grinning again!" His grandfather was glaring at him from the end of the long narrow downstairs hall. "If something's so funny, *share it*. It's rude to be having your own private jokes and excluding people like that. What are you smiling about?"

Oliver felt as though he were tied up in chains. If he said nothing, his grandfather might get even madder. If he explained his grin, he'd be in even bigger trouble. But at that very moment, rescue came flying down the stairs in the form of his mother. He'd never been more glad to see her.

"Quick, Oliver!" she was saying. "Up you get to your room and get your things unpacked. It's almost time for bed, and you have a lot of things to do tomorrow before school on Monday." He tore up the stairs as though shot from a gun.

School! He was glad to escape his grandfather's fierce eyes and dangerous question, but he'd completely forgotten about school. His steps slowed as he approached the room that he and Jerry would be sharing. New kids. New teachers. New things to learn. He stopped short as he reached the bedroom. Jerry was in the middle of the floor, standing on his head.

"Hi, Oliver!" said the cheerful voice coming from the hooked rug. "Just thought I'd see if this new life of ours would look any better if I looked at it upside down." Oliver laughed. Jerry could be wild and crazy, and he had the shortest fuse in Moose Jaw. But from time to time he could be more fun than a roomful of monkeys.

* * *

Later on, Grandpa left the house to go to the local variety store to pick up some milk for next day's breakfast. Oliver heard him go out. Here was a good chance to go down to the living room and see his mother before bedtime. Maybe just seeing her would make him feel better.

But as Oliver approached the living room from the steep stairway, he could see that the TV was turned on. And his mother was plunked down in front of it.

So nothing had changed. Before leaving Moose Jaw it had been like that. Night after night, she'd sat facing that darn TV set, hunched up on the sofa, with her fist pressed hard against her mouth. Oliver sat down on the step and watched the program.

There it was — all the same scary stuff. Pictures of missiles exploding in mid-air over Israel. Views of wounded people on stretchers. And terrible dead bodies. Men in uniforms — big important soldiers with their chests full of ribbons — saying how accurate their bombs and missiles were. Heartbreaking pictures of cormorants limping under the weight of spilled oil. The sad frozen faces of prisoners of war.

Oliver closed his eyes and plugged his ears with his two fingers. Then he turned around and walked slowly upstairs. When he reached the second floor, he didn't stop. He trudged on up to the third floor and looked around at the boxes and trunks and assorted junk.

Oliver searched the attic for two things he wanted — a blanket and a comfortable place to sit. He found a faded and torn antique chair with a blue velvet seat and back — ripped and shabby, but soft and comforting. Then he found an old plaid picnic blanket in a big plastic bag, took it out of the mothballs and dragged it over to the chair.

Wrapping himself in the blanket, Oliver curled up on the chair and let himself think about all the things he needed to think about. His father and the danger he might be in. The Gulf War, and what it meant to everybody. This strange, almost foreign city, with its steep hills and painted wooden houses. The harbor, which was only six blocks from this house, and which he'd like to have a closer look at. His stern grandfather. His mother, who suddenly was acting like a daughter — and sometimes a cross one — instead of a mother. Jerry, who was fun one minute and mad the next. His strange silent grandmother, who seemed to be nervous and sad. School, and whatever it would bring.

Oliver sighed, and two tears slid down his cheeks. It was safe to cry up here. No one would scold him or make a fuss over him or tell him that boys don't cry. Not up here.

Oliver looked around the attic, and felt his heart lift a little. This was already his refuge — the place he could come to for sorting things out if the going got too rough. "A place to go," he whispered. "Somewhere to escape to." The limbless dress form looked like an old and comfortable friend; so did the ancient dolls and the toy trucks.

As he walked down the stairs, he could hear that the grownups were leaving the living room. He could hear his mother saying, "Well, at least I don't have to worry about Oliver. He's steady as a rock. And as calm as a millpond."

Oliver shook his head as he closed the door to the bedroom, and climbed into bed. Well, he'd try not to disappoint her. But it would be nice if just once in a while he could try being himself, instead of someone they wanted him to be. Just himself. Whoever that might be.

Four

Mrs. Kovak offered to accompany the twins to Tower Road School on Monday, but Jerry refused to let her come. "Arrive at school with our *mother*? Huh! That'd really fix us. I can just hear the things the kids would say about *that*. C'mon, Oliver. We're supposed to get there early on the first day. Get a move on!"

It wasn't far to the school, and the directions their grandfather had given them were easy to follow. Oliver wished it were farther. It was a foggy morning, and the muffled sounds of foghorns drifted up from the harbor, mixed with the hollow sounds of boxes being dropped or shoved around on the wharves. Ghostly shapes appeared out of the heavy mist and then were swallowed up by it again. It was mysterious and interesting, and Oliver wished he could walk around in the fog all day. Besides, if he did that, he wouldn't have to be going to this new school. When he heard the sounds of kids' yelling and laughing in the school yard, he felt even worse. There must be a billion kids out there, he thought, and I don't know even one single one of them.

Oliver and Jerry walked right through the yard full of kids and into the school. Jerry looked as though someone were forcing him to jump into a pit of fire, but his head was high and his shoulders back. Suddenly he turned and glared at Oliver. "Totally unfair," he said. "Why can't I be like you?"

Oliver frowned. "What dumb thing are you talking about?" he muttered.

"Calm. You're always so darn calm," snapped Jerry. "Doesn't anything ever *bother* you? Don't you ever *feel* anything?"

Oliver felt a wave of helplessness sweep over him. First his mother. Now Jerry. Even his father. How could they have lived with him for twelve years and still not know him?

"I do!"

"Do what?"

"I do *so* feel things."

"Huh!" scoffed Jerry. "I just bet that if a missile exploded across the street right now, you'd still go on walking into the school with that stupid blank look spread all over your face."

How do you explain to someone that you can be blank on the outside and a churning cauldron inside? *Cauldrons* — Oliver had heard that word for the first time on TV, about a month before. He'd learned they were huge pots, often made of iron, and that in stories they were used by witches for boiling oil and other hot and bubbly stuff. That's exactly what his insides felt like — as though they were a black cauldron full of foaming hot liquid. Oliver smiled as he thought of this.

"And Grandpa's right about that secret sneaky smile of yours. It's rude. It shuts people out."

Oliver wanted to explain about the boiling cauldron.

"I was just thinking about —" he began.

"Oh, forget it!" growled Jerry, his voice thin and hard. "Just *forget it*!"

Right in front of them, not far from the school entrance, was a door of frosted glass, with a sign painted on it. It said:

MRS. OGILVIE
Principal

Oliver knocked. A voice called out, "Come in!"

Mrs. Ogilvie was seated behind a huge desk strewn with papers and notebooks. She was a small woman, quite young — about their mother's age — with dark brown hair, a round face, and large tortoise-shell glasses.

"The Kovak twins," she said, and stood up. Even when she was standing, she looked tiny behind that desk. But there was something strong and direct about her eyes behind the big glasses, and Oliver knew that this was a person you'd never try to deceive. He figured if he talked back to her, she wouldn't need to say anything. She'd just *look*, and quick as a flash, he'd be sort of flattened against the wall, as sure as if he'd been struck by a laser beam.

"Welcome!" she said, and smiled a wide wonderful smile, before she came around the side of the desk and shook hands with both of them. "I have all the documents from your old school," she went on, "so I don't have to waste your time with questions. Let's go right up to your home room while it's still quiet in here. The bell's going to ring any minute, and then there'll be a stampede — something you boys probably know all about."

But even before she'd finished her sentence, the loud electric bell was sounding throughout the school, and the stampede had started.

* * *

On the way to their classroom, Oliver had a chance to look around. Although he was still uneasy, he was able to notice that this school was different from any he'd ever been in. For one thing, it was old. Instead of tiles and metal and plastic, it had a lot of smooth polished old wood on the bannisters, around the long stairway, and surrounding the windows and transoms on the doors. There were odd little hallways and short unexpected staircases leading to unknown places. It was strange and unfamiliar, but somehow warm and comforting. You knew that kids had been coming to this school for many, many years. And they'd survived. You didn't *die* from going to this school. Not instantly, anyway. He grinned at that idea.

So, when the door to the classroom opened, Oliver was wearing his strange secret smile, and Jerry was frowning so hard that he looked as though his face might crack wide open.

"Class," announced Mrs. Ogilvie, "I'd like you to meet Oliver and Jerry Kovak. They're from Saskatchewan, and I hope you'll make them feel welcome in their new province and school." Then she said to the home room teacher, "They're all yours, Mr. Blanchard." She flashed them her broad smile again, and was gone.

Mr. Blanchard did all the right things. He welcomed them to the classroom, then told the class that the twins were here in Halifax because their father was away at the Gulf War. Way back in August, long before the war had started, many of the children had gone down to the waterfront to wave off the ships heading for the Persian Gulf. One of the boys jumped out of his seat and said, "My dad's at the war, too."

Then Mr. Blanchard did the wisest thing he could have done. He just gave Oliver and Jerry some textbooks and notebooks, and left them sitting there, paying no attention to them at all before recess.

Oliver leafed through the books to see if they looked too hard. They looked fine. Then he watched what was going on in the classroom. Mr. Blanchard was an interesting teacher — sometimes even funny. The kids didn't look like monsters. And it would be nice to meet that guy whose father was also at the Gulf War. Oliver began to feel a lot safer. By the time the bell rang for the break, he was starting to think that he might just possibly live through this day — maybe even through the whole term.

Out on the playground, it looked at first as though things were going to work out okay, too. One boy looked at Jerry's tallness and his wide shoulders, and said, "You a good skater? We need someone to play defence on the class hockey team." Jerry went off with him and joined a knot of kids over by the outdoor rink.

Then Oliver saw the boy who'd said his father was at the war, too. He was short and stocky, with a broad chest and a thick mop of dirty blond hair. He was coming towards him in a sort of marching, purposeful way. Good, thought Oliver. A new friend. But as he approached, a girl from the class whispered to Oliver as she passed by, "Watch out for Gus. He's the class bully. He'd tear the tail off his own dog. And he's always got a pack of wolves with him."

As Gus and his friends came closer, Oliver could feel the cauldron starting to bubble up in his stomach again. But Gus was smiling and shaking a friendly fist. "My dad's a gunner," he said. "He's the one who shoots the guns out of them planes." Then he said, "What's your father do in the army? Or air force? Or what?"

Oliver swallowed and took a deep breath. "In the army," he said. "He's a nurse."

"A *what*!" Gus stopped walking, and just stood there with his mouth hanging open.

"A nurse. He's part of a field hospital."

Gus let out a harsh laugh. "A nurse! Hey, guys! Listen to this! This kid's father is — guess *what*! — a nurse!" His laughter was loud and ugly. "Does he wear a white skirt, or what? What a sissy stupid thing for a man to be doing in a war. My old man, now, he's shooting down planes every chance he gets. That's what a war is all about — shooting." Then Gus raised both his arms, pointed his index fingers, and pretended to shoot down everyone in the group.

"You're dead! You're dead!" shouted Gus. "Lie down, you dummies!" And suddenly, all Gus's gang dropped down onto the ground and closed their eyes. Gus made as if to put his guns away.

"There!" he said. "We won the battle. And that's the way my dad does it. Brave and strong, killing everything in sight." Then Gus sneered. "While your father tiptoes around a stupid hospital, making beds and plumping up pillows. Nothing but a silly old nurse."

Oliver was ready to break through his shyness and let fly with what he really felt. He wanted to stand up for his father so badly that he didn't even feel scared of Gus and his gang. He had a lot of things he was dying to say. Like: Armies do a lot of things besides shooting and killing. One of the things that our forces have always done best is keep peace, and save lives. Or: My dad is braver than yours, because he doesn't have a whole airplane full of guns to protect him. Or: Who do you think is gonna look after your father if he gets wounded or sick? Or: In wars, they *need* male nurses. They need them to push around heavy beds and to lift huge men.

Oliver was ready to say all those things. No. He wasn't ready. He was *willing* to say those things. He wasn't frightened of Gus or anyone else at that moment. He wanted to defend his father, supposing the whole school yard turned against him.

But to Oliver's horror, he discovered that his throat was too tight to speak. He knew that if he started to say anything, he'd burst out crying, right in front of all those kids. And that was something he couldn't or wouldn't do. Not even for his father. And it was thinking about him that was pushing Oliver so close to tears.

He just stood there and clenched his teeth together and dug his nails into the palms of his hands. He could feel the silence like a weight on his head as the group of kids waited for his response. He stared at Gus, until Gus finally gathered together his pals and led them away. "Sissy nurse!" he shouted back, just before they disappeared around a corner of the school.

Suddenly, Oliver was aware that Jerry was in the crowd that had been watching. The hockey team kids were grouped around him, and Jerry was looking red and embarrassed. Embarrassed about what? About Oliver, for just standing there and not defending his father? Embarrassed about his father's job? *What*? Then he heard Jerry say:

"That's my brother over there. He's made of cement. Nothing ever bothers him."

The bell rang for the end of recess. Oliver sighed and started to walk slowly towards the school entrance. His throat was loosened up by now, but it was too late to be of any use to him.

When he entered the school, he almost bumped into the principal, who was standing in the hall. Her face lit up with her bright smile, but he didn't even see her. He knew he had never before in his whole life been so unhappy.

Five

O n his fourth day in Halifax, Oliver woke up to another gray day — fog, and what the radio weatherman was calling intermittent drizzle. This time the fog didn't look so mysterious and wonderful. But the bacon smelled good, and Oliver rushed to put on his clothes and join the others downstairs.

On the other side of the kitchen, Oliver could see Jerry looking out the window, shoulders drooping. "Some winter!" he exclaimed. "People around here must have a lot of fun skiing on the bare sidewalks."

"Too much complaining around here," snapped Grandpa, shaking out his morning paper.

Oliver looked at his mother to see her reaction to all this, but she was rushing too hard to notice very much. It was the first day of her new job, and she was nervous.

Oliver watched his grandmother as she went to and fro in the kitchen, serving bacon, pouring coffee, making toast. He liked his grandmother, but she seemed to him to be sort of wishy-washy. Yes dear, no dear, to her husband, no matter what cross thing he was doing — and never looking really happy. And his grandfather was forever telling everyone else what to do and how to do it. Right now, he was in the living room turning up the sound on the TV, so that he could hear the war news in the kitchen.

"Isn't that maybe a bit loud, dear?" murmured Grandma, but her husband didn't even answer her. Then he spent most of their breakfast time growling — about the neighbor's barking dog, about Jerry's foot kicking under the table, about the toughness of the bacon, about the weather. And right through the complaints, Oliver could hear the TV set blaring out information he didn't want to hear. He wished he could put a soundproof bag over his head, so that he couldn't hear or see those exploding missiles, those people running and yelling, those planes roaring off through the night sky.

And Jerry was strange and distant all of a sudden — no headstands in the bedroom *this* morning. Oliver thought he knew why. He figured that Jerry must be ashamed of him. On that very first day of school, Gus and his gang seemed to have decided that Oliver was either peculiar or a fraidy cat. Probably Jerry agreed with them.

But now, on his second day at school, Oliver had a dim hope that he might be able to fix up all those things. He was scared, but he half hoped that Gus would stop him in the school yard and say the same things to him that he'd said the day before. This time, he was sure he'd be able to explode with all the things he really felt.

But when Oliver reached the school yard, he could see that Gus and his gang were over in the little kids' section, leaning on the play equipment, talking. When they saw Oliver, they were suddenly silent, looking over at him. But they didn't come nearer. Gus yelled, "Sissy nurse!" and started prancing around the jungle gym with little, mincing steps. Then they all ran off behind the school, and Oliver could hear them laughing.

Oliver thought about laughter — how it could make everyone feel warm and comfortable inside, if it was the right kind. But if it was the ugly kind, it was one of the worst sounds that anyone could hear.

It was after school that day that the snickering started. As Oliver walked into the yard, the group over by the play equipment started to snicker. It's hard to cope with a snicker, because there's nothing definite to deal with, no clear answer to give. Oliver went over and over in his head the things he wanted to say to Gus if he ever made fun of his father again. But all he ever got from him from then on were those dumb snickers. And sometimes, from too far away to answer, those two terrible words: "Sissy nurse!"

When he was older, Oliver looked back at this time in his life, and it seemed to him that he had been trapped in a hole that was getting deeper and deeper with each passing day. By the end of the first week in Halifax, he felt as though there was no one nearby who could help him climb out of that hole.

Sometimes, when he walked to school in the morning, Oliver let himself remember the old days in Moose Jaw. They seemed to him like a sort of heaven. He'd had lots of friends who understood his quietness and even admired him for it. Both his parents were home on most evenings to talk to and watch TV with. Jerry always seemed to be there and ready to spend time with him. A nice house. Nothing to worry about.

Of course, Moose Jaw hadn't really been *perfect*. But now everything was all messed up. His father was gone. That was the worst part. And the war news was so scary that it made his chest feel like a cave, with a cold hard stone in it. His mother had started her new job and was at work every day, but even in the evenings, she seemed to be off somewhere else, locked up in her own head. Probably worrying about the war, thought Oliver. Or else she was looking daggers at her father or having arguments with her mother.

Mr. Blanchard was a good teacher, and Oliver found his classes lively and often fun. But Phys. Ed. classes were a nightmare for him. He'd always had difficulty with games that involved objects — pucks, balls, sticks, bats. He couldn't seem to get it all together. Where others hit and caught, Oliver missed and fumbled. Out in Saskatchewan, he'd tried and tried to improve those skills, but no kind of practice or training seemed to work. This broke at least one corner of his heart, but the Phys. Ed. teacher there had seemed to understand his problem, and no one made fun of him or tried to push him farther than he could go.

Not so here. On the fourth day after their arrival in Halifax, Jerry and Oliver joined the other kids in the gym for a class with Mr. Hennigar, the hockey coach and Phys. Ed. teacher. Mr. Hennigar was sturdy and muscular, with powerful arms, an army-length haircut, and piercing eyes.

On that day, there were relay races involving various ways to handle a basketball. The kids passed it between their legs, over their heads, and threw it to appointed team members.

"I want that passing to be accurate!" yelled Mr. Hennigar. "And no dropping!"

While the gym rang with the shouts of the boys, Oliver endured the torture of doing almost everything wrong. It was as though the ball were covered with grease. Again and again he dropped it, and when it was his turn to throw it, he seemed unable to make it go in the right direction. During the times when he had to wait for his turn, he noticed two things. He saw Jerry doing everything right — catching, throwing, intercepting. And he saw Mr. Hennigar looking back and forth between the boys — grinning at Jerry, scowling at Oliver.

At the end of the session, Mr. Hennigar announced in a loud voice, "Welcome to the Kovak twins from Moose Jaw. Jerry, you're a natural. I can see that you'd be an asset on any team. Oliver — it's time you got off your butt and practised your skills. This class is no tea party. If you can't even catch something as big as a basketball, you'd better start trying a whole lot harder. Class dismissed."

Hockey practices were even worse. Mr. Hennigar made fun of him or yelled at him for all the things he did wrong — his passing, his receiving, his shooting — ignoring all his good points, such as his speed and flexibility. At the very first practice, Mr. Hennigar called him over to center ice and said, "Look,Oliver. I don't just come here for fun, you know. I'd rather be home watching TV and resting up for tomorrow. But I give my time to you kids after school hours so that you can have a good team. How about *you* trying to give something, *too*. At the moment, you're more of an obstruction than a hockey player."

Gus was a whiz at passing and shooting, and Jerry was good at almost everything that happened on ice. More and more, Gus and Jerry became Mr. Hennigar's favorite students. He never seemed to get tired of telling them how good they were. "Good work, Gus!" "Terrific pass, Jerry!" But then: "Oliver! Could you try to hit that puck just *once*?"

Mr. Hennigar wasn't only the hockey coach. He was also the Health and Fitness teacher. This meant that Oliver would be faced with Mr. Hennigar once a day, either in the gym, at the rink, or in the classroom. When Oliver discovered this, he could feel a lasso tightening around his stomach. "One stomach ache per day," he muttered to himself as he walked home from school that day. "Five days a week. Until the war is over."

When he reached home that day, he asked his grandmother, "How long was World War II?"

"Six years," she answered. "Why?"

"Just wondering if my stomach will survive," he said. His grandmother gave him a look that was both puzzled and troubled. As he went upstairs to put away his books, he sighed. Six years! If the Gulf War lasted that long, his stomach would be like an old limp piece of charred rubber before it was over. Oliver grinned when he thought about that.

Things didn't get any better as the days went by. Mr. Hennigar had made up his mind that Oliver's only problem was laziness. "*Work*!" he kept yelling at him. "*Try*!" He couldn't see that there are some things that some people just *can't do*, no matter how hard they try.

Mr. Hennigar didn't know about all the hours Oliver's dad had spent trying to teach him how to play hockey — hockey being the game that Oliver wanted most to be able to play. Finally his father had said, "Look, Oliver. Being able to manoeuvre a puck around the ice isn't that important. It's not the most special thing in the whole world. There are a lot of other things that you do well. You draw well. You swim like a fish. You're a nice kid. So, relax. When you're ninety years old, it won't matter to you whether or not you were the best hockey player in grade five or grade seven or grade nine."

But that hadn't satisfied Oliver. He wasn't ninety years old right then, and he wanted to be on the school hockey team.

Then his father had tried to make him see that there are sometimes things that you just have to *let go of*. "I can play hockey," his father had said, "but I can't draw. And no amount of lessons could make me a good artist. You can draw really well, but you can't seem to handle a hockey stick, no matter how hard you try. It just seems like your eyes and your hands can't get together on it. I guess it's something your body just doesn't want to do. Or can't. I'll help you whenever you want to practise, but try not to torture yourself over it."

So Oliver had learned to accept the fact that he was never going to set the hockey world on fire. And now it seemed that he was supposed to unlearn that very hard thing that he had come to accept.

Then one day, in Health and Fitness class, Mr. Hennigar announced the subject of their term project. The title of the assignment was to be "Baseball — Then and Now". As the kids all bent down to write the title in their notebooks, Oliver could hear someone whisper, "Baseball! Mr. Hennigar's favorite sport. Better not slip up on *this* one!"

Oliver sat up straighter in his seat. Here was his big chance — maybe his only chance — to change Mr. Hennigar's attitude towards him. Maybe, thought Oliver, if I can write the best report of my entire life, Mr. Hennigar will realize that I'm alive — and maybe even worth something. And certainly not lazy.

The more Oliver thought about the project, the better he wanted it to be — not just *his* best report, but the absolute best baseball report in the whole class. He'd *force* Mr. Hennigar to respect him.

Six

All that week, Oliver worked on his report in every spare moment he could find. Grandpa complained that he wasn't doing his share of the chores. "Oliver," he'd say in that cold, hard voice of his, "if *I* were someone's guest, *I'd* be thoughtful enough to be helpful around the house." But Oliver would just mutter, "Homework. Sorry," and then disappear upstairs. Half the time he had the room to himself, because Jerry was at the rink so often, practising with the hockey team. Other times, Oliver worked in his secret place in the attic, or in the school library.

Oliver loved the time he spent in the library. It was a large square bright room, lined with books, and in one corner there was a huge comfortable sofa. When he was reading up on background material, he could curl up on that sofa and forget all about the bad things in his life — Gus, Mr. Hennigar, his grandfather, the war. Mrs. Rosen, the librarian, was helpful when he needed to find material, and always knew where to look for information.

Other good things happened in the library, too. All during the previous week, Oliver had noticed a red-headed boy watching him. He'd never seen a face so full of freckles. Every time Gus or his gang yelled, "Sissy nurse!" or snickered, the boy would screw up his eyebrows in a troubled frown. And now he was in the library, working on a project for another class. On that first day when Oliver started his own report, they were the only two people in the big room.

"Hi," said the boy. "I'm Harry O'Reilly."

"Hi. I'm Oliver Kovak."

"Yeah, I know. Everyone knows you're Oliver. Because you're new. And because Gus is out to get you."

Oliver grinned. "A great way to get famous."

They both sat down on the big sofa.

"Everybody's scared of Gus," said Harry. "Some kids pretend they're not, but they are. All of us are."

"Nice we've all got something in common," said Oliver, and Harry chuckled.

"What're you working on?" asked Oliver.

"A project on swimming. It has to be called, "Swimming As a Sport — How It All Began." History stuff. I love swimming, but I can't seem to find many books on it. And Mrs. Rosen is at a staff meeting".

Oliver reached over and pulled a book off the shelf. "I just noticed this," he said, "when I was looking for something on baseball. It's a neat book. We all read it in our swim club out west. Great diagrams of how to do the different strokes. And two whole chapters on the background of swimming as a sport. Have a look."

Harry's face lit up. "Way t'go!" he exclaimed. "Thanks a lot. How about you? Find any stuff on baseball? I know a couple of really great books. I like baseball almost as much as swimming."

Oliver grinned again. "Not me. I'm denser than the bat. If you can't hit anything or catch anything, it's hard to be in love with baseball. And that's a pretty good description of me."

"Then why choose to write about it?"

"We didn't get to choose. We got *told*. And I have to write the best report of my life. To make Mr. Hennigar think I'm smarter than Einstein. Mr. Hennigar and Gus are in competition to see who can hate me the hardest." Oliver laughed.

"Well," grinned Harry, "you're not exactly describing my two favorite people. Let's go find those two baseball books, and then maybe look for some more. Mr. Hennigar thinks that heaven is made up of a whole bunch of baseball diamonds, all strung together."

All week long, Harry and Oliver worked in the library. Mrs. Rosen helped them, and they helped each other. At the end of each day, they'd walk home along South Park Street and Victoria Road. An *ally*, thought Oliver. Wars aren't quite as bad if you have an ally.

* * *

The report was due on Friday at 3:30 p.m. Oliver finished it during his lunch hour on Thursday. He'd worked eight long days on it. And nights. He flipped through the pages, closed it up, and patted the cover. That afternoon he took it to school, just to make sure he wouldn't forget to take it to class the following morning. He grinned to himself. As though he could forget!

Oliver thought about his project as he walked along. He felt like the world's authority on baseball. He chuckled to himself at that idea. But he'd spent long enough with encyclopedias and other source books in the library to know that all his facts were on target. And he'd added some graphs and tables to make it look extra special. Oliver had seen his uncle — his dad's brother — doing that kind of thing when he'd done essays in college. "Sort of puffs them out," his uncle had said; and he always got good marks for his work.

On the way to his classroom, Oliver met the principal, Mrs. Ogilvie. "Höw's it going, Oliver?" she asked.

"Great!" said Oliver, and meant what he said.

Mrs. Ogilvie threw him one of her electric smiles. "I'm glad," she said, and continued on her way.

Oliver put his report inside his desk, and then went outside with Harry.

"Listen, Oliver," said Harry. "I told my swimming coach about you. I said you knew a whole lot about swimming and were good at it."

"I never said I was good at it," said Oliver.

"Yeah. But I bet if you know all that stuff you must be at least *some* good. Are you?"

Oliver paused before he answered. "Yes," he said. "Not bad." He laughed. "Not like in hockey or baseball. No balls or pucks in swimming. Nothing to catch or throw."

Harry seemed excited. He went on, "So the coach said why didn't I bring you to the swim club on Saturday. We could have fun. Not just in the pool. But afterwards. Or before. And we do other things besides race at the swim club. We learn lots of new strokes, too. And diving."

Oliver grinned. "Sounds great," he said. Things are looking up, he thought, as the bell rang.

"Race you to the basketball post," said Harry, and they were off and running. Oliver won. They fell down on the ground, laughing. Yes, things *were* looking up. Oliver suddenly realized that he hadn't thought about the war for two hours.

* * *

The next day when Oliver woke up, he thought, this is The Day. The day Mr. Hennigar gets my project. He whistled on his way to school, and just laughed when Jerry told him he was off-key, and to shut up.

That morning, in gym class, they had relay races involving stick-handling. Oliver actually smiled when Mr. Hennigar started yelling at him to keep his eyes on the puck and to *try*! Today's special, thought Oliver, and there's no way anyone's going to make me feel miserable.

"Look at him smiling," whispered Jerry to one of his friends. "He doesn't seem to care what anyone says or does to him. Weird!"

To Oliver, the day seemed almost too good to be true. Gus was away from school with the flu, and with him gone, Oliver felt all the misery go out of him. He and Harry played tag and talked and hung around, and there was no one there to snicker or to mutter, "Sissy nurse!" as he walked by. The members of Gus's gang weren't even hanging out together. With him gone, it seemed that they'd lost all of their ammunition.

Then, when Oliver came in from recess, he reached in his desk to feel his report. Just to feel it, he told Harry later. Just to feel good about it being in there. *And it was gone.*

The fear that shot through him was a real physical pain. It started in his stomach, and then shot up into his chest and then down into his legs. He could hardly stand. Frantically he pulled all the books out of his desk and went through them — once, twice, three times. *It wasn't there*.

For the rest of the afternoon, Oliver lived through his classes in a kind of trance. He didn't ask any questions, and he didn't answer any that were directed at him. He just sat there like a stone statue, staring straight ahead, scarcely breathing. Thinking about his father and the war, thought Mr. Blanchard, and didn't disturb him. When the bell rang and everyone raced out of the room to practices and clubs and home, Oliver continued to sit there, his mind numb and empty.

Finally, Oliver moved out of his trance, and went off to the washroom. He thought of all the hours he had spent on the research and writing of that report — of his beautiful charts and graphs, of the way he'd written it out three times, just to make sure it was really neat, to make sure it was *perfect*. And then he thought of how happy he'd been all day, knowing that at last that dragon, Mr. Hennigar, would know that there was at least one thing he could do well. And now he didn't even have a *bad* report to hand in. Mr. Hennigar would kill him.

When he returned to his classroom, Oliver couldn't believe what he saw. There it was — the report — right there on his desk, with the cover facing him as he entered the room.

He didn't take the time to wonder what had happened. Maybe the caretaker had found it. Maybe a strong wind from the window had blown it out of his desk. Maybe — who could tell? He didn't care. He just grabbed the report and raced up to Mr. Hennigar's office.

"Late!" growled the teacher, as Oliver placed it on his desk. "When I said 3:30, I *meant* 3:30. All the other assignments were handed in on time. Five marks off for lateness. Some people just never manage to do anything right."

Oliver was still so relieved to have found the report that none of Mr. Hennigar's words bothered him. He raced out of the school and ran most of the way home. Now all he had to do was wait until Monday afternoon. Then he bet his whole world would turn around. He couldn't have cared less about those silly five marks. And in the meantime, there was the swim club on Saturday to look forward to. He knew his mother would let him go.

Before he went into the tall blue house that day, Oliver looked up, and the sky was filled with a thousand seagulls. A pretty strange sight to see in the middle of a city, he thought. But nice. He looked hard at the high flat-faced house. Well, he thought, it's *interesting*. He listened to the sounds coming up from the harbor — the hoots and chugs and whistles — and noticed the smell of salt and tar in the air. I could get to like this place, he realized. Today, I'll keep away from the TV set, and pretend there's no war on. Maybe I can even make myself believe it.

Seven

On Saturday, Harry called for Oliver, and they walked together to the YMCA on South Park Street. Beyond the Y loomed the Halifax Citadel — a high bald hill with fortifications on the top and a moat around it. "In the summer," said Harry, "there's a really neat museum open up there, and it's fun walking along the edge of the moat and rolling down the hill."

Once inside the Y, Oliver felt at home. As he took his shower, it seemed to him that all Y's looked alike and even smelled the same. The smell of chlorine was like an old friend, and as soon as he dove into the pool, he experienced the familiar pleasure of moving through the water with speed and with skill.

"Look at that new kid go!" yelled one of the swimmers. Another one called out, "Now we can finally beat Truro in the Spring Meet!" Harry shouted, "If you think he's good at the crawl, wait'll you see him do the butterfly!" Oliver felt as tall as a giant, and as strong as Goliath.

Then, when he returned home for lunch, his mother was there, full of tales about her new job and about the people she worked with. Even she seemed to have forgotten about the war for an hour or two. Then she looked at him carefully, and asked, "Are you okay, Oliver? Is everything going well at school?"

And Oliver answered, "It's okay, Mom. I'm fine. Everything's fine."

Why did he keep doing that? he wondered. Was it to save his mother from worrying about him? Or was it because he really did feel pretty good about things, today? Or did he want her to go on thinking that he was strong and brave? If she'd asked him the same questions the week before, maybe he'd have been frantic enough to have told her everything. But today was different. Funny thing, he thought, when you don't even know for sure what you're thinking or why you're thinking it.

Then his mother said, "I really appreciate the way you can cope with things without falling apart, Oliver. I'm not in too hot shape myself these days. Your dad's absence is terrible for me. And I'm not very good at pretending to be a daughter again, instead of a mother and a wife. *And* a red-hot computer expert," she added, with a grin.

"And Jerry's all tangled up inside," she went on. "He's mad and sad about the war, and worried about his father. He doesn't know how to deal with all those feelings, so he just acts angry at other people. He's forever slamming doors and kicking things, and I'm really worried about him." She put her arms around Oliver and gave him a big hug. "So it's nice to know," she said, "that there's at least one person I don't have to worry about."

All this made Oliver feel proud and warm inside. It also made him feel uneasy. He didn't really *want* to be that strong. He didn't *want* her depending on him. Well — in fact, he *did*. But he also *didn't*.

Sunday was all right, too. Grandpa growled around a lot, but he also told some interesting stories about Nova Scotia during the Second World War, and this made

Oliver feel a bit better about his own fears over the Gulf War.

Grandpa said that during that war, there were so many armed services people in Halifax and Dartmouth that often you couldn't turn in any direction without seeing at least one person in uniform. Sometimes the kids bet each other a nickel that they could do that. And usually they lost.

Those servicemen and women weren't just from Canada, either. There'd been American gobs with their white sailor hats, and the Free French sailors with their red pompoms. There were blackout curtains and air-raid sirens, and searchlights streaming across the sky at night. Bedford Basin was always full of ships — often hundreds of them — and they seemed to be from almost every part of the world. Sometimes, from far off, you could hear gunfire, and you couldn't help wondering what it meant, or if it would get any closer. Oliver listened, fascinated, and tried to picture in his mind exactly what Halifax must have been like back then.

He could see that Grandpa was an interesting man, who had it in him to be a really wonderful person. But, like Jerry, he was scared stiff of appearing to be weak. Both of them would a thousand times sooner be unjust or mean than act weak in front of other people. Or maybe even in front of themselves.

It seemed to Oliver that everyone in the house was wearing a mask. And his own mask covered up who he really was as much as the other family masks covered up the real people behind them. Pretty interesting, Oliver thought, and then grinned.

"There's that kid doing that damn secret smiling again," growled Grandpa.

Then his mother snapped, "Smiling doesn't happen to be a federal crime, Dad."

In the living room, the TV blared on and on. Certain words emerged out of the welter of sound: " . . . gas masks . . . Scud missiles . . . ground forces . . . land mines . . . casualties . . . prisoners of war." Oliver tried to close his mind, but he couldn't close his ears.

* * *

But now it was Monday, the day he'd been waiting for. And the morning was bright and colorful in the clear vivid way he'd become used to on sunny Nova Scotia days. As he walked to school, he felt as though his feet were hardly touching the ground. The sky was cloudless, an intense blue, and the paint of the wooden houses shone in the sun. On the many trees, there was a faint powdering of snow. He knew that Halifax was known as The City of Trees, and this morning the white branches made him feel like he was walking through a magic frosty planet. For the day to be this beautiful must be a good sign, he thought.

Today there had even been some good things on TV. This morning he'd heard the announcer saying, "No allied casualties last night." So he could stop worrying about his father for a few hours. The bad things usually happened at night.

Last evening, Oliver had wondered how you prayed about this war. If you prayed that the Coalition forces would win, it meant that thousands and thousands of people on the other side might die, or get hacked up in various ways. How could you pray that kind of prayer? Some people didn't care if those people died; some even *wanted* it to happen. But when Oliver shut his eyes and thought about the battlefield, terrible scenes flashed onto his mental screen. He knew he couldn't pray for any of those things to happen. So he just prayed that the war would end — and fast. Never mind the details about *how*. Maybe some really smart politicians or soldiers could *talk* themselves out of it.

Oliver sighed. His mind got all fuzzy and tangled up when he tried to work these things out in his head. He wanted everything to be simple and quick. But he was old enough to know that things very seldom work out that way.

In school, the day seemed to drag along with weights on its feet. He wanted it to be the last period — Health and Fitness class. That's when Mr. Hennigar would come into his classroom, hand him back his report, and say, "Well done, Oliver. You did a phenomenal job on that project." *Phenomenal*. Oliver wasn't sure what that word meant, but it sounded like something he'd like to hear.

In one of Oliver's daydreams, Mr. Hennigar went on to say, "I'm sorry, Oliver. I misjudged you." But Oliver knew that this was a lot more than he could ever expect or hope for. Besides, he didn't need anything that good.

At last it was time for Health class, and for the first time, Oliver looked forward to the arrival of Mr. Hennigar. Then the door opened. In he came, his arms piled high with class reports.

Mr. Hennigar put the papers on his desk. Then he stood in front of the class and folded his arms. His eyes were cold, and his voice, when he spoke, was gravelly and stern.

"Today I have a sad announcement to make," he began. "Someone in this class has done a sneaky and dishonest thing. And this I will not put up with. Ordinarily, when I have to scold a kid, I take him aside so that the class won't be watching. But today, I want him to be an example to the whole class of how not to behave."

Oliver raised his eyebrows. He thought of how often he had been scolded by Mr. Hennigar in front of other people. He felt sorry, already, for what that kid would soon be feeling.

There was a lot of foot-shuffling going on in the room, and paper-rustling. What was he going to say? Who was the class villain, and what awful thing had he done?

Then Mr. Hennigar spoke. "Someone in this class is a cheat. And I know who it is. A student has taken somebody else's report — stolen it — and then copied the whole thing out, word for word, sentence by sentence."

He turned and looked straight at Oliver. "No wonder," he said, "that you were late turning in your report. You must have needed that extra time to copy it all out — so neatly, so perfectly. You took Gus's report, and after you copied it, you turned in the exact same assignment. Even the charts and graphs. I can hardly express my disgust."

Oliver stood up. He was too full of rage to be scared, and there was no rope around his throat, preventing him from speaking.

"I did *not* copy that report!" he declared, his voice loud enough to reach the next room. He was almost yelling. "That was my *own* report. I am *not* a cheat. I worked over a week on it. *I didn't copy it!*"

Then Oliver sat down. He could feel that awful thing rising up in his throat, and he thought, if I cry right now, in front of all these kids, I'll die.

Then Mr. Hennigar started handing out the reports, talking all the while he was doing it. "Let's not add lying to your other shortcomings, Oliver," he said. "I happen to know how lazy you are . Your skills are terrible, and you don't even try to improve them. Gus always does good work — in the gym, on the rink, in the classroom." Then he said, in a quiet, threatening voice, "I guess we know who needed to get a good mark in this class. I guess we all know who cheated on this assignment."

Oliver looked at the mark on the front page of his report. It was a large red zero, which covered half the page. As he looked through the other pages — so carefully written and re-written *three times* — he saw that Mr. Hennigar had drawn an angry red slash through every page — through all his charts and tables, even through the inside title page.

For the second time since coming to this school, Oliver found that he was unable to speak. He stood up again. He glared at Gus until he raised his eyes from his report and looked up. Oliver stared at him for a full half minute. Then he looked at Mr. Hennigar. He couldn't get any words out, but he hoped that both of them were able to hear what his eyes were saying. He knew that if he didn't escape from this room, something inside him was going to explode.

Oliver picked up his books and stalked out the door of the classroom, down the long stairway to the school entrance, past the big front door with its stained glass window saying Tower Road School, and then out into the empty school yard. He walked home, went in the front door, and climbed straight up the stairs to the attic room. He closed the door carefully, sat down on the torn velvet chair, and pulled the blanket around him and over his head.

Then, at last, Oliver let it all out. He cried harder than he had cried since he was three years old. When you're a three-year-old, you can cry like a howling dog. And that's pretty much what Oliver sounded like. He cried for his father and for his fears for him. He cried for his old friends and his new enemies. He cried for a strange house in a strange land. He cried for the way the triumph of his project had turned into a terrible defeat. And he cried for all the sad and unjust things in the whole world.

If anyone had been in that house, they would have heard him, in spite of his being so far away and buried under the blanket. He made that much noise. But no one was home. When he finally stopped crying, he fell fast asleep. When he woke up, at five-thirty, he felt as though he had been on a long, long journey. And he wondered how much farther he would have to travel before he reached his destination. He was very, very tired.

Eight

The next day, Oliver walked home for lunch by himself. Jerry stayed behind to find out more about hockey practices, and he didn't even act very friendly when Oliver asked him if he was ready to leave. Harry had a dental appointment. All the way home, Oliver kept kicking pieces of ice ahead of him, kicking, kicking, until he started to feel a little bit better. But not very much. Mainly, Oliver felt so miserable that he could hardly bear it.

He thought about the stories that his grandfather had told about the giant explosion during the First World War, when much of the city had been destroyed. And about the smaller one in the Second World War, when most of the enormous munitions magazine on Bedford Basin had caught fire and blown up. Thousands of people from Halifax and Dartmouth had left their homes and spent the night on beaches and in fields in safe, faraway places. But if an explosion happened this afternoon, Oliver thought, I'm not sure I'd even notice it. He'd maybe try to tell his mother how he felt when he got back to the blue house.

But of course Mrs. Kovak wasn't there when he reached home. She was downtown, working at that new job of hers. He'd forgotten about that. His grandmother let him in, and took him out to the kitchen to get his lunch.

"How was your morning?" she asked.

"Fine," he said. *No. It was awful, awful, awful. Every time I close my eyes, I can see my assignment with the red slashes all over it. And probably everybody thinks I'm a cheat. Not just Mr. Hennigar. Maybe even Jerry.*

"Good!" she said. "Your mom told me to expect that. She said that Jerry might be upset, but that you'd be fine. That's the word she used. 'Fine.' Good for you, Oliver."

Well, if she thought he was so darned fearless and heroic, he certainly couldn't tell *her* his problems.

Oliver ate up his soup and sandwiches at the kitchen table, with his grandmother looking on. "I'll have my lunch later," she said, "when your grandfather gets back from his walk."

"Where's he walking?" asked Oliver.

"Oh, I don't know," she said. "Anywhere. The Park, maybe. He's kind of at loose ends now that he's retired. Hasn't got any hobbies. Doesn't know what to do with himself." She looked hard at Oliver, as though trying to decide whether or not to say something.

Then she said, "That's probably the reason why he's so cranky these days. I think he misses his friends from work. And probably feels kind of useless. He was always in charge of a lot of things. Now he's not in charge of anything."

"But . . ." Oliver didn't know whether or not he should ask this question, but suddenly he had to know. "But I heard Mom ask you why you didn't stop his crankiness way back when she was a little kid. And you said you were afraid the family would all be at war with each other if you tried to do that. So . . . was he cranky back then, when Mom was a kid? Or wasn't he? He wasn't retired then. I don't understand."

Grandma smiled. "No, he wasn't retired. He was at the other end of his working life. And he found that hard, too. He was just starting out in his work, and he was full of so much ambition that it nearly ate him alive. So he worked too hard and worried too much, always hoping he'd get to be big and important." Grandma stopped, and put her fist up to her mouth. "I never told anyone these things before," she said.

"Go on," said Oliver. "Tell me some more. Maybe then I'll understand him better. I won't tell. Honest."

Mrs. Fraser got up and started to clear the dirty dishes from the table. She moved as though she were tired, and her eyes looked troubled as she worked. Finally she stopped stacking plates, and came back to Oliver and sat down.

After a moment, she went on. "Well," she said, "if you're sure it'll just be between you and me . . . Anyway, your grandpa's ambition was terrible. All we ever wanted from him was just to have a kind and happy man in the house. We didn't need him to be the big boss at work. We didn't ask to be eating steak at every meal. We just wanted things to be peaceful." She sighed. "But that wasn't enough for him. He wanted to be the president of his company. And he never rested for five minutes until he was."

"And then what happened?" Oliver was scared he'd be late for school, but he didn't dare let Grandma stop speaking, in case she never got started again. He didn't know she *could* talk this much. And he was learning interesting things. "Was he happy then? Did he get to be more peaceful?"

"Yes, he did." Grandma smiled. "He never got to be what you'd call *easy* to live with, but he stopped being such a bear. He did a lot of kind things, and he was very good at his job. Even I could see that. The people who worked for him respected him, and the company did well. He was successful and he was important. A very big toad in a small puddle. He liked that."

"And now?"

"And now there's nothing to organize, nothing to create, nothing to sell, nothing to advertise — no challenge, no deadlines. And no one to boss around." She chuckled. "Except us. And he found out just how small a puddle he'd been head toad of. His pension is small, so he's not even free to cut loose with money. He doesn't say so, of course, but I think he feels like he's right back where he started. That must be hard to take when you've been running the show for fifteen years."

"Yes," said Oliver. "*Boring*." Then he said, "I'm glad you told me all that stuff."

"And it was kind of nice to get it off my chest," said Grandma, "although I feel guilty for telling you all those heavy family secrets."

"Sometimes it's hard to tell anyone your secrets," said Oliver. "I bet it feels real good."

"It feels wonderful," she said. "I don't know why I told you all that, but I'm glad I did. Maybe it's because you're a good listener. Lots of people can talk. But not everyone's a good listener. Your father's one of the best listeners I know."

Oliver sighed. "I know. I miss that. And a lot of others things." He paused. "What about Mom?"

"Well, she probably listens to *you*. Some, anyway. But she's not too crazy about listening to me. She thinks I should have been able to stop your grandfather's temper tantrums. She blames me for them almost as much as she blames him. Maybe more. Both my children do."

"But you really couldn't stop him, eh?"

"No. I feel so sad about that — but no, I couldn't. I was too frightened of him, and I never did learn to be brave about other people's anger. I was afraid that if I fought back, he'd get even madder, and then take it out on the children. Or if I let them fight back, that he'd stop liking them. He didn't like anyone who stood in his way. But . . ."

"But what?"

"But it seems like that's what they wish had happened. They think it would have been simple. They have no idea how complicated it all was. So they think I'm a wimp. And I guess maybe I am. But it makes me unhappy that they think that." She was making little ridges in the tablecloth with her fingernail.

Oliver reached over and patted her hand, "I don't think you're a wimp," he said. "I think you're brave."

"*Brave*!" Grandma was astonished.

"Sure, brave. It's real hard to tell the things that are messing you up inside, and you've just gone and done it. I call that brave."

She laughed. "Well, maybe," she said. "But it shouldn't have taken me thirty-five years to spill those beans. And now that my children are grown up, I should be able to stand up to anger a little better. It's funny I chose a twelve-year-old boy to tell my life story to. I think perhaps it's because you seem so much like your father. Jerry, now, he's more like your mother — a bit prickly and not always working things out clearly in his head. But you and your father seem to me to be kind of level and wise." Then she touched his hand and said,

"Thank you, Oliver. I'm glad you've come to live with us."

Oliver had a lot to think about as he walked back to school that afternoon. So she thought he was like his father, eh? He loved that idea, even though he didn't really think it was true. He was probably more like his grandmother — a little bit wimpy, and finding it hard to get his fears and his worries out in the open. Grandma had opened up something for him. He wasn't sure what it was, yet, but he knew that he felt better than before she'd talked to him. For a little while he forgot about the war, and Gus and his gang, and the way Jerry was acting so strange. He even forgot about his assignment for an hour, and Mr. Hennigar.

Oliver looked around him as he walked along. He was getting used to these strange wooden houses with their elaborate porches and broad verandas. Even today he was able to recognize that he was starting to like this city — the pungent salt air, the hilly streets, the tall trees. The sun was glistening on the newly fallen snow, and he could hear the boats hooting and chugging down by the harbor. Already he loved those sounds. This place was beginning to speak to him with many voices.

Nine

T he next day, a special teacher came into the classroom to teach art lessons. Her name was Miss Menski. Oliver could hardly wait for her to unpack her paper and paints and crayons. Drawing was a skill he was good at. It would be nice to succeed at something for a change. In gym class that morning he'd felt like he'd had two left feet. Even before the big mess about the baseball report, Mr. Hennigar had picked on him. But now it was worse. They'd been playing dodgeball, and for Oliver it had been torture.

"Are you *really* Jerry's brother?" Mr. Hennigar asked. "His *twin*? Just look at *him*! He's a natural-born athlete. I don't expect everyone to be that good, but you could at least keep your eyes open and keep track of the ball. You could *try*. This game happens to be *easy*."

Oliver had wanted to shriek at him, "Maybe for *you* it's easy! Not for me! And I *am* trying! But I *can't do it*. My eyes and feet seem to be at war with each other." There was that word again. War. War. War.

But now there was going to be an art class, and this was one thing he always felt at home with. He could draw like a whiz. He'd show that Gus guy. And this hour would also be a chance for Oliver to forget the war for a while. It seemed that it was the only thing anyone talked about anymore.

The teacher laid out the art materials on the front desk, and then she announced, "I want you to draw a special picture today. I'm going to ask you to make a picture of the war. Each of you can do it in your own way. You can use any materials you choose, and you can draw anything you want. It can be disgusting or scary or orderly or confused or whatever you want it to be. Anything you want."

Oliver couldn't believe it. Was there nowhere he could go without that stupid war spoiling everything? He felt mad at the teacher and the war and the school and almost everything he thought about. He marched up to the front of the room and grabbed some paper, some crayons, and three Magic Markers.

At the end of the hour, Miss Menski collected the pictures, and hung them all up on the wall. Some kids had drawn soldiers marching, airplanes with bombs dropping out of them, families watching TV sets, ships sailing out of the harbor with men lined up along the decks. But when she put Oliver's picture up beside the others, everyone gasped. It seemed to be just a collection of shapes and lines and colors, but it was strangely beautiful. Miss Menski looked at it for a long time after she'd put it up. Then she spoke. "We only have time to talk about one picture today, and this is the one I've chosen. The name on the bottom is Oliver. But I guess he must be new, because I've never met anyone with that name before."

She looked out at the class, and said, "Oliver?"

Oliver answered, "Yes. Me."

"Oliver," said Miss Menski, "do you suppose you could tell us something about your picture? It's beautiful, and it's what we call an *abstract painting*, but I think we need you to explain it to us."

Oliver suddenly felt his shyness fall away from him. He loved drawing, and he didn't mind talking about it, because he always felt on solid ground whenever he drew or painted. He knew what he was talking about.

"Okay," said Oliver. "I used three colors — red and gray and black. The red is for anger and hate and all those other bad feelings that are happening in this war. I put gray in because I think gray's a sort of sad color. I feel gray a lot when I think about the war. I guess that families with fathers or sisters or brothers in the war often feel gray all over."

"And the black?" asked Miss Menski.

Oliver went on. "The black is there because I think fear is black. Black is the same as darkness, and darkness is scary. Death is black, too."

Oliver stopped, while Miss Menski waited for him to continue. Finally, she said, "Anything else?"

Oliver took a deep breath. "And the shapes mean things, too," he said. "The big red blobs are blood and other angry things. The jagged lines are fear lines, and the gray circles are for rain and tears."

Then he sat down. He couldn't believe he'd said all those things. In fact, he wasn't even sure he *understood* what he'd said. But he looked at the picture and liked what he saw. He could see that there was good balance in the color and shapes, and that somehow or other he'd made a beautiful thing out of a lot of ugly feelings. And he could hear kids around him saying, "Ever neat!" "I like his picture best" and then, "Can we all do pictures like that next time, Miss Menski?"

The bell rang to signal the end of the school day. Before Oliver left the classroom, Miss Menski asked him to stay back and speak to her for a few moments. When everyone else was gone, she told him to sit down.

Then she said, "The war bothers you a lot, doesn't it, Oliver?"

"Yes," he said.

"Why?" she asked.

"Lots of reasons," he said. "But one special one."

"Which is?"

"My dad's over there. In the Gulf. I'm scared that all the things I hear about on TV are going to happen to him."

Miss Menski spoke quietly, "What does your father do in the war, Oliver?"

"He's a nurse in a field hospital," said Oliver.

"Oh, Oliver!" she said. "You must be so proud of him."

"Yes," he said, and he could feel his throat tightening up again.

Miss Menski looked at him with such kindness that he had to look away and stare at his hands. "Do you get a chance to talk about how you feel?" she asked.

"No," said Oliver. "It's like someone taped my mouth shut. Besides . . ."

"Besides?"

"Besides, my mom and brother think I'm calm and strong and that nothing bothers me. It even makes my brother mad. So it's real hard to explain how awful I feel. When they ask me how I am, I just say, 'Fine.' That seems to be what my mother wants to hear. That way she can think I'm a lot like my father. Besides, I guess I don't really want to stop seeming so brave and cool."

"You could write it all down," suggested Miss Menski. "In a diary, or in letters to someone. Your father, maybe?"

"No. I couldn't write that stuff to my dad. It would make him sad to have to worry about those awful things I'm thinking."

"You could write him letters, and not send them," she said. "Then, when he comes home, you could give them to him. Or not. Whichever you wanted."

Oliver just looked at her. He was clobbered by how good he felt when he heard those words: *You could write him letters and not send them*. It was as though someone had opened up a door and let a cool breeze blow into a hot stuffy room.

"A sea breeze," he said.

"Pardon?" said Miss Menski.

"Just like a sea breeze," repeated Oliver. Then he chewed his lip and looked as though he were trying to decide something. Finally, he said, "Miss Menski?"

"Yes, Oliver."

"Have you got a car?"

"Yes," she said. "Is there somewhere you want to go?"

Oliver grinned. He could feel the door opening wider and wider. "I want to see the sea," he said. "I'm from the prairies, and I want to see what the sea does to the sky. We have such big skies out west, and I miss them. Is the sea far away? Could you drive me there?"

Miss Menski picked up her briefcase and put on her coat. "We can be there in less than five minutes," she said. "This is one of the things that make Halifax and Dartmouth such wonderful places to live in. C'mon. Let's go."

Four and a half minutes later, Miss Menski parked the car down by the Container Port, at the edge of Point Pleasant Park, and both of them got out and stood by the sea wall. Neither of them spoke.

Oliver looked out at the sea, blue and bright in the winter sun. Past the rocky point on the right, past the lighthouse on Meagher's beach, past the huge tanker that was entering the harbor, stretched the horizon.

Oliver breathed a deep sigh of relief. It was almost the same feeling he'd had when looking at the endless fields of wheat on his own prairie. He felt he could travel straight ahead forever, and never reach the end of what he was looking at. And the sky was huge. Why had no one told him it would be like this?

"Thank you," he said to Miss Menski. "I think maybe I'm gonna be okay. Maybe not right away. But sometime."

* * *

That night, Oliver wrote a letter to his father. He told him about the plane ride, the blue house, the wooden bannisters in the old school, his first view of the sea from Point Pleasant Park, about swimming with Harry, about his abstract picture. He put that letter in an envelope and stamped and addressed it.

Then Oliver wrote him another letter. This is what he said.

Dear Dad,

It's better here than it used to be. But often it's still awful. The gym teacher says I'm a klutz. He also says I cheated and that I copied my assignment from Gus. So probably everyone else thinks I'm a cheat, too. And I'm scared of Gus and his gang. Gus. What a dis-gus-ting name. And I wish Jerry was like he used to be. Most of all, I'm worried you'll get killed or wounded or something.

> *Love,*
> *Oliver.*

Oliver put that letter in an envelope, sealed it carefully, and put it in his bureau drawer underneath his T-shirts. He felt better. Not *all* better. But some.

Ten

Harry called for Oliver next morning, and they walked to school together. The previous week's snow was melting in the February thaw, and the boys splashed through the slushy gutters, enjoying the mess they were making of themselves and the sidewalks.

"Listen, Oliver," said Harry, and then stopped.

"What?"

"Listen," Harry began again. "I know you didn't copy that assignment. I saw you working on it in the library. I was there. I saw you dumping the first two copies in the wastebasket. And then I saw you making the third. I know — we both know — who did the copying. But . . ."

"But what?"

"But I can't tell on him."

"I know." Oliver kicked a piece of ice across the street.

"The worst criminal in the world is a tattletale. I'm not scared of Gus." He paused. "Well — not *very* scared. But, holy! A snitch is worse than a cheat."

"I know."

"If I told on Gus, I might just as well move to Sir Charles Tupper School. Everyone would hate me. Teachers included."

"I know." This time, Oliver threw a big chunk of ice against a tree. He threw it so hard that it broke into dozens of pieces.

"I'm sorry," said Harry.

"C'mon!" cried Oliver. "Race you to the school." And they took off, splashing icy water in all directions. They were soaked when they arrived at school.

* * *

That day at recess, Harry had to stay in his classroom to correct an assignment. When Oliver went out into the school yard alone, he could see Gus and his gang over by the fence. Gus was staring at him with his thumbs in his ears, waggling his fingers. He was far away, but Oliver could hear the distant words clearly. "Sissy nurse! Sissy nurse!"

There wasn't any danger of Oliver's throat choking up this time. He was so mad at Gus that there wasn't any room in his head for sorrow, and certainly not for fear. He was so full of rage over the assignment that he didn't care if Gus and his gang tore him apart, limb from limb. If he were ever going to make that speech to Gus, it had better be now, while he was still feeling all those things. And if Gus was never going to come close enough for Oliver to tell him off, Oliver would have to go to *him*.

Oliver ran across the school yard, and stopped when he was right in front of Gus. He'd spent so much of the day before rehearsing his speech, that when he spoke, he didn't even have to stop to think about what words to use.

"Okay, you two-bit twerp," growled Oliver, "you and I both know who did the real baseball project. If you were half as brave as that hero father of yours, you'd go and tell Mr. Hennigar the truth. You make me want to spit."

And then Oliver actually spat on the ground. He could hardly believe he'd done it. But he had, and it made him feel great.

A crowd was gathering. This might shape up into a show worth watching, and no one wanted to miss it. Gus was lounging against the fence post, staring lazily at his fingernails. His gang stood around snickering.

"What did you buy your old man for Valentine's Day?" sneered Gus. "A white apron? To tie over his skirt? Some soldier! Before I'd let on that my dad was a *nurse*, I'd lie about what he did. A sissy nurse!"

Oliver could feel a sort of blinding white flash inside his head. He was so mad that he wouldn't have been afraid to step on a land mine. He moved closer to Gus and grabbed him by the front of his jacket.

"If you ever call my father a sissy nurse again, *I'll kill you!*"

"Step right up," said Gus, eyes lazy, still staring at his fingernails. "Do it. Kill me. Lots o' kids here to witness the event."

But Oliver wasn't finished. "Who do you think is going to look after your dad if he gets wounded? Some little tiny girl nurse? If your father is as big as you say he is, it'd take six girl nurses to lift him. But my dad's real tall, and strong as a bull. That's why they need men nurses in the army. To lift and turn and carry all those heavy men. And to push big stuff around."

Oliver let go of Gus's jacket, and went on talking. "And my dad's ten times as brave as yours is. Your father has guns and missiles and planes and ships to protect him, but when my dad's inside the tent, he doesn't even have a gun. He just has himself. But that's all he needs. That's how brave *he* is. Besides, it's not such a sissy thing to do, to be spending your days and nights saving people's lives."

Then Oliver looked hard at Gus for a few moments before adding, in a voice that was as loud as a yell, "*So you just shut up!*"

Gus continued to inspect his fingernails, but his gang wasn't snickering anymore.

Then Oliver turned around and walked through the crowd back to the school entrance. Somewhere in the middle of the group he glimpsed Jerry. He was grinning. As Oliver passed within earshot, he could hear him say, "That's my brother, Oliver."

* * *

When Oliver reached the blue house that afternoon, everyone was out except his grandmother. She was watching TV, and as he opened the door, Oliver could hear the sounds of explosions, and voices talking about gas masks, warheads, casualties, nerve gas, germ warfare. When his grandmother saw him, she turned off the set.

"Thanks, Grandma," said Oliver. "I hate all that stuff. Scares me to death."

She looked at him sharply. "It does, eh? Everyone — your mom and Jerry — they all say that nothing bothers you. But I've been wondering. I figured you just might have a few little fears and worries tucked away somewhere inside you."

"Right on!" said Oliver, grinning. "Lots of them. And Grandma," he went on. "Guess what?"

"What? Tell me."

"I blew my stack today. I told off the school bully. I may get killed for it, but right now it sure feels good. And you know what else?"

"What?"

"You and me are a lot alike. I'm not like Mom, and not like Dad, even if some people think I am. And I'm not like Jerry or Grandpa. But I *am* like you."

She laughed. "Oh, Oliver!" she protested. "You're not. You're the brave one around here. I'm the wimp."

"I'm not brave," said Oliver. "I'm just holding everything in. Stuffing all those things way down inside me, so they can't get out. Like you. Until today. Today I feel a little bit brave. Like you did yesterday, when you told me all those secrets." He grinned at her. "If we stick together," he said, "maybe we'll both stop being so wimpy."

Before they could say anything more, the front door opened, and Grandpa came in, stamping the snow off his feet.

"Snowing again," he said. "And a terrible wind. Stupid damned weather! It can't decide what to do. One day it's cold enough to freeze an elephant's ear. The next day it thinks it's spring. Not healthy. And today we've got a real storm brewing."

Then he frowned, and said, "Who turned off the TV set?"

His wife took a deep breath, and said, "I did. It's not easy for Oliver and Jerry to be watching that war news all the time. It's no picnic for the rest of us either. It's like the war is being fought in our very own living room." She stopped for a moment, and looked at her husband's angry face. She swallowed. But then she continued, "We don't need to know about every single bomb that falls, or every prisoner that gets taken. We could try reading the newspaper instead. Or," she added, "you could watch the black and white set in the bedroom." She was standing straight and tall, chin up, looking her husband in the eye.

Oliver watched her. Nothing wimpy about *her*. He was reminded of that afternoon in the school yard. The wimp and the bully, with the tables turned. He and his grandmother grinned at each other.

"So!" snapped his grandfather. "Hmph! I'll just remind you about one thing. This happens to be my house."

"And *mine, too*," said Grandma. "And it's my opinion that all those war programs are too hard on the boys. They're not as old as we are, you know. And their father happens to be over there where it's all taking place."

Mr. Fraser just stood there in the hall, dripping snow onto the rug, saying nothing.

Finally he said, "If you're going to be so blasted bossy about it — okay. I'll go upstairs and watch. Just this once. Just for today. But I don't know who you think you are, telling me what to do."

Oliver went over to his grandfather as he leaned over and started to take off his boots. It was worth a try.

"Lookit, Grandpa," he said. "I've been down to the Container Port by the Park to see the sea. I love it down there. There's still some light left in the day. I'd like to see what it looks like in a storm. Could we go down, right now, and watch it for a while? Could we?"

His grandfather straightened up. "A walk, you say? Sure! We've both got our outdoor clothes on, so we can start off right this minute. How about a couple of cookies before we go, Grandma? Fuel for our tanks."

And then, cookies in hand, they started off.

* * *

Down at the water's edge, the wind was whipping the harbor into whitecaps, and two tugboats were tossing around in the waves like a couple of bath toys. The snow was blowing across their vision at an angle, and the trees were bending against the wind. Without thinking, Oliver grabbed his grandfather's hand, and looked up at him, eyes shining through the snowflakes in his eyelashes. "Hey, wow!" he yelled above the noise of the surf. "Ever great! This sea stuff is as good as the prairies." Then he said, "Hey, Grandpa?"

"Yes, what is it?"

"Could we come down here often? You like to walk, and this seems like a real neat place to do it. I'd like to come and walk with you. I bet it's really something in the summer."

His grandfather cleared his throat. "Well. Well, yes, I suppose so. Yes. It would be nice to have the company. Gets lonesome, sometimes. Maybe on the weekend. We'll see."

And through his mittens, Oliver thought he could feel his grandfather give his hand a small squeeze.

Eleven

U sually Jerry started off for school long before Oliver, so that he could get in a half-hour of hockey practice before classes began. But the morning after Oliver and Grandpa's walk to the waterfront, the practice was cancelled; so the boys walked to school together.

"Really gave it to him yesterday, didn't you?" said Jerry, as they walked along the slippery sidewalk. There'd been rain in the night, and the snow had turned to ice. Every so often they'd do a run on it, then slide for half a block. Or it seemed that far.

"What?"

"Gus. You really gave it to him."

"Yeah. I guess so. Today he'll probably kill me. But I don't care. Much."

Jerry shook his head. "I wish I could be like you," he said. "You seem to have it all figured out. Sometimes you just don't seem to care about anything. That must be kind of restful. I always care. And I'm mad most of the time these days. But this time . . ."

"This time, what?"

"This time you did care. So you gave it to him. Right to his face. Holy! How could you be that brave? I'd be scared to death to stand up to him. That's why I kept pretending I wasn't listening when he'd yell those awful things about Dad. I got enough things to worry about right now — cranky old Grandpa, Mom nervous as a cat, Dad at the Gulf, living in such a stupid house. I sure don't need to be wondering if I'm going to be dead before recess is over. I'm so jealous of you that sometimes I want to kick you."

"*Me*? Jealous of *me*? *Why*?"

"Cool. So damn cool. Mom thinks you're the Rock of Gibraltar."

"Well, I'm not. Not cool. Not the rock of Gi-whatsit. And I do care. It just doesn't show. It's all piled up inside me like a lot of compressed garbage — or dynamite." Oliver chuckled.

"And always laughing or grinning when people are talking about serious or awful things. *Why*? That *really* bugs me."

Oliver scratched his head. "Beats *me*," he grinned. "It's just that every once in a while something strikes me funny — right in the middle of some crisis or something. I can't help it. It just happens. Maybe there's something wrong with my funny bone. Deformed or something." He laughed.

Jerry laughed nervously. "Well, I sure don't get it. But it must be nice. To be able to laugh and all, while this war is going on. When Dad could be killed any minute. Or worse. Like get nerve gas sprayed all over him. Or have his arms blown off. And I can't say any of that stuff to Mom. She'd do all that heavy sighing, or else start crying or something. Then I'd have to worry about *that*, along with everything else."

"So you just get mad and kick things around." Oliver laughed. "Well, I guess it isn't any worse than freezing up like an icicle. Like me."

Jerry stopped in his tracks and looked sharply at Oliver. "Do I really do that?"

"Do what?"

"Kick things around?"

"Sure you do. Well — sort of. You know — hit things, slam things, get mad if anyone even looks at you sideways."

They started walking again, and Jerry didn't say anything at all for a while. Then he said, "It's not fair what I said about Mom. She tries to get me to tell her how I feel. But holy! If I told her how I really felt, about Dad and the war, she wouldn't be able to sleep nights for the next six months — or however long this stupid war is gonna last. So she just winds up saying" — and here Jerry mimicked her voice — "'Jerry *dear!* Do try to *calm down!*' It makes me real crazy when she does that."

Then they were at the school yard. Oliver looked around nervously. He wasn't feeling quite so brave anymore. But he didn't see Gus anywhere. Not even over by the tire swing, where he liked to hang out with his gang before school. Oliver took a deep breath. Maybe this was going to be a holiday for him.

"The enemy," he said to Jerry, "has gone undercover. If we're really lucky, we'll find out that he's sick with something long lasting — like scarlet fever or the plague." Then Oliver turned to Jerry and said, "See ya," as he set off across the yard to talk to Harry.

Sure enough, Gus *was* absent from school. Or, thought Oliver, gone away just long enough to copy out someone else's assignment. He frowned. It would be a long time, he knew, before he would forget that big red zero on the front page of his project, or the red slashes through every page. He sighed. Most of all, he hated it that Mr.

Hennigar thought he was a cheat. And probably whole bunches of other people thought so, too.

Just my luck, thought Oliver. Phys. Ed. was first period. Floor hockey. Just as bad as ice hockey, without the fun of being on skates. He wondered if Mr. Hennigar was going to be out to get him for the rest of his life.

And it seemed as though that was how it was going to be. Mr. Hennigar moved among the players with his whistle dangling from his mouth. Every so often he'd take it out, and yell, "Oliver! Go after that ball! *Hit* it! Oh, for gosh sakes, can't you do *anything* right? *Try* for a change!" Or he'd say, in his loud raspy voice, "Oliver Kovak! What's *wrong* with you? If I threw you something the size of a beach ball, you'd still manage to miss it!"

What *was* wrong with him? wondered Oliver, as he slowly walked over to the bleachers for time-out. Why could he draw, but not catch a ball or dribble a puck or hit a softball? Why could he do some things with his hands and feet, and not others? Why could he swim so well, and yet be so klutzy on the gym floor? He frowned deeply, and hardly noticed when Mrs. Rosen, the school librarian, entered the gym, her arms piled high with books.

"Some cattle fodder for you, Fred," she called out to Mr. Hennigar. "Those booklets on floor hockey that you asked for. Just came today."

"Great!" exclaimed Mr. Hennigar, all smiles. "Some of these kids really need to read up on the sport. Like Oliver Kovak, for instance. He doesn't know a stick from a lawn mower."

Mrs. Rosen chuckled. "But he probably knows more about baseball than you do," she said.

"*What*?"

"Yeah. No kidding. As you probably know. You must have read his assignment by now."

"What assignment — ?" Mr. Hennigar looked uneasy.

"The one he was working on in the library all last week. Never did see a kid so determined to write a perfect report. Wrote it out three times before he was satisfied with it. Guess you haven't read it yet, or you'd know what I'm talking about. Wait'll you see his charts and graphs! As the kids say — *awesome*!"

Mr. Hennigar frowned. "Are you *sure* about that? Did he *really* do that?"

Mrs. Rosen snorted. "What do you mean, am I sure? For one whole week, and more, he practically lived in the library. I suggested to him that he might like to bring in a tent and some cooking utensils." She let out a big laugh, and disappeared out the side door of the gym.

Oliver had heard most of what had been said. So had the rest of the kids in the class. He looked at Mr. Hennigar, who seemed to be drawing an invisible picture on the gym floor with his toe. A small figure appeared at the door. It was Mrs. Ogilvie. She stood there, serious, puzzled, trying to figure out what was happening in the silent gym.

After what seemed a very long time, Mr. Hennigar finally looked up, and came over to where Oliver was standing.

"I seem to have done a very terrible thing," he said to him. Then he took a deep breath. "I owe you an apology, Oliver. I'm really sorry. It's bad to cheat, but it's even worse to accuse somebody of cheating unless you're sure of the facts. Now — where's Gus?" He looked around the gym. "Not here today, I guess." Then he went on,

"Bring your assignment back to my office at three-thirty, and I'll change the mark. I think I gave you a pretty low one."

"Zero," said Oliver. *And put red slashes all over every page.* But suddenly it struck him as funny. "No way to go but up," he said, and chuckled.

Mrs. Ogilvie smiled quietly, and then disappeared from the doorway.

When Oliver went up to Mr. Hennigar's office at three-thirty, he put the assignment on his desk, and waited. Mr. Hennigar looked at the large zero on the cover. Then he slowly leafed through the project, through page after page of red slashes. Finally he closed it, put his elbows on the desk, and covered his face with his hand. He stayed that way for a long, long moment.

"Oliver," he said at last, "I've been giving you a rough time. I'm sorry. But nothing is as bad as this. I gave Gus ninety-five for his assignment, and I'll be changing that to zero. But I'm giving you a hundred. I never give a hundred to any essay or exam, but I never received a project that was so well done. There's not one thing wrong with it, and there's a whole lot that's close to perfect."

Mr. Hennigar went on. "So I'm going to give you five extra marks, as a sort of consolation prize for messing it up. Besides" — and here he grinned at Oliver — "it's the only way I can think of to change all those slashes into something pleasant."

Mr. Hennigar then took his red crayon and put a huge 10 in front of the zero on the first page. Then he put two giant zeros after each slash, until every page was decorated with a large red 100.

"All is forgiven?" asked Mr. Hennigar.

Oliver thought that maybe he should be satisfied with this one victory. And in a way, he was. But in another sense, he wasn't. "Sure," he said. "But Mr. Hennigar . . ."

"Yes, Oliver?"

"I *do* try in hockey. And in floor hockey. And in softball. If you think I'm bad in hockey, wait'll you see how awful I am in softball." He grinned. "If there was a trophy for Worst Player of the Year, I'd win it every year."

Then Oliver sobered up. "Mr. Hennigar," he said, "I think maybe there's something wrong with me. Something to do with my body and maybe my eyes. Sometimes they can't seem to work together. Not with things that move. My dad tried to teach me all those things — hockey and softball and stuff — and I tried really hard to learn, for years and years. But I couldn't. And I don't think I'll ever be able to. And I'd like it if—" Here Oliver stopped. It was one of the longest speeches he'd ever made, but he didn't think he could finish it.

"You'd like it if what, Oliver?" pressed Mr. Hennigar.

Oliver took another deep breath. "I'd like it," he said, "if you'd stop telling me I'm lazy. And making fun of me in front of all those kids." Then he added, "I *am* a good swimmer. I can draw. I'm not stupid at *everything*."

Oliver discovered that his T-shirt was soaking wet. He could tell by the feel of his face that he was beet-red. His heart was going clang, clang, clang. But he felt as though another door were opening.

Mr. Hennigar rose from his desk and put out his hand. "Shake on it," he said. And they did. "I'm a changed man. Or I hope I am. If not, I'll work on it. I'm going home for the evening to practise being human for a change. I've been a dragon long enough. By Monday morning, I may be unrecognizable."

Then, as Oliver prepared to leave the room, Mr. Hennigar spoke again. "What's your dad do, Oliver? Why did you move to Halifax?"

"He's in the army," said Oliver. "He's a Captain. He's a nurse. He's in the Gulf War."

"A nurse, eh?" said Mr. Hennigar. "You must be very proud of him."

"Yes," said Oliver, "I am." Then he turned quickly and left the room. He could feel that thing happening in his throat again. Be darned if he was going to stand there and cry all over his assignment.

* * *

That evening, Oliver climbed up to the attic so that he wouldn't be able to hear the war news on TV. There he wrote a long letter to his father. This time he didn't have to write two long ones. He had a lot of things to say that his father would be really happy to hear. After he'd sealed and stamped and addressed the first letter, he wrote another one — a short one.

Dear Dad,

I'm feeling better, but I'm still afraid of Gus. He'll be a raging lion when he discovers that Mr. Hennigar knows who cheated on the project. I'm scared of what he'll do. But most of all, I'm sad about you being away. I'm afraid you'll get killed or wounded. It's hard to be happy, even when good things happen.

Love,
Oliver.

Twelve

On Saturday morning, Oliver walked over to the YMCA with Harry. It was a sunny morning, almost like spring, so they took a long, long route, going right down to the harbor before they started up Sackville Street.

Oliver had never been down to that part of the waterfront before. They watched a huge container ship moving out to sea, and snooped around the old wharves, admiring the sparkling water in the harbor, and the ferry boats chugging back and forth between the two cities.

"This is really a neat place," said Oliver, as they started the long climb up to South Park Street. "I maybe still like Moose Jaw best, but it sure could use one of *those*" — and he pointed across the road to where the Halifax Citadel rose high above them with its star-shaped moat and the Old Town Clock built into the side of the hill that faced the sea. "There's so much *old* stuff here. I like that."

They passed the Royal Artillery Park on the left, and rounded the corner by the CBC building. Then, as they turned into the Y, Oliver looked across at the Public Gardens, where last night's new-fallen snow was still sitting on the tree branches. "I bet those gardens are really something in the summer," said Oliver.

"They are," said Harry. "Lotsa flowers, being a garden and all, and fountains and a little river and statues and ducks and a million pigeons. People walk through them on their way to work. Sort of a long cut instead of a short cut."

Oliver grinned. Everything looked good to him this morning — the weather, the blue sea, a friend to enjoy things with, and the memory of those 100's written all over his assignment. And now, in a few minutes, swimming.

That day, his time for lengths was his best yet, and the coach praised him. "Almost ready for that meet in the spring," he said. "You're small, Oliver, but you're wiry and fast. You tear through the water like a rocket. We're really glad to have you on the team."

Oliver thought about his hockey coach, and then he thought about his swimming coach. He laughed out loud, and left the coach wondering what on earth was so funny. But people were starting to get used to Oliver grinning or laughing for no apparent reason.

He left the pool and went off to have his shower before dressing. "I like today," he shouted to Harry, who was in the next stall. Then he muttered to himself, in a voice that no one could hear, "I even think I'm starting to like that crazy blue house."

* * *

When Oliver reached home, it was almost lunch time. His mother was helping his grandmother make sandwiches, and Jerry was pacing around the large kitchen, too hungry to sit still.

"You two guys are taking forever to make that stuff," he growled, and his mother answered, cheerful but firm, "If you're in such a big hurry, Jerry, no one's going to complain if you make your own." But Jerry just kicked a chair and stomped off upstairs. Oliver followed him.

"What's up?" he asked, when they were in their room.

"It's Grandpa," said Jerry, chewing on his thumbnail and then pitching a ball of paper at the opposite wall. "He thinks he's gonna die if he doesn't watch TV every minute of the day. He plays it so loud that you can hear it, no matter which set he has on. Says he has to be *informed*. It drives me crazy seeing all that stuff. All those weirdos in their gas masks. Besides —"

"Besides what?"

"Besides, I've heard people say that Halifax could be a danger spot for terrorism. Why don't *we* have gas masks?"

Oliver sighed. "I dunno, Jerry," he said. "I guess they think we're not gonna need them. Maybe they have too many other things to worry about. They're probably too busy doing stuff over *there* to think about things happening over *here*." Oliver paused. "I guess that's not much help," he said.

"No! It's not!" snapped Jerry, and stormed off to the bathroom.

Oliver sat on the edge of the bed and stared into space. He'd said to Jerry that "we're not gonna need them." But he hadn't really had time to think hard about it. Now he did. He wondered if Halifax *was* as safe as he'd thought. After all, there were all those ships in the harbor, particularly that big one that they were outfitting to send to the Gulf. And there was Shearwater Base on the Dartmouth side, with all those aircraft sitting around waiting to be bombed. And the Stadacona Naval Base down by the harbor. Nerve gas. Germ warfare. What kinds of things happened to you if you ran into that stuff? And what about an explosion? Oliver swallowed hard. If they could have two explosions, couldn't they have three? He sighed again. "Something else to worry about," he said out loud.

* * *

That afternoon, Oliver went down and stood beside his grandfather's chair. On the TV screen were pictures of the prisoners of war who'd been captured weeks ago. Their faces looked so sorrowful and sort of — what was the right word? — *stunned*. Oliver shivered. He didn't want to think of his father looking like that.

"Grandpa," he said.

"Yes? Yes, what is it? Speak up, child. I'm busy."

Oliver cleared his throat. "It's nice out. Sun and all. Snow on the trees. And warm for February. I thought —"

"Thought what? Come on. Out with it."

"I thought maybe we could go for a walk in the Park."

His grandfather grinned. "Hoped you'd say that," he said, and rose to switch off the set. "Meet you on the front steps in five minutes."

Oliver hesitated. Then he said, "Could Jerry come, too?"

Mr. Fraser sighed. "That kid's like a pea on a hot griddle. Can't keep still for five minutes. No peace in him, at all. And cranky as all get out."

Oliver grinned. *Just like you*, he thought.

"But . . . all right" said his grandfather. "I suppose he can come, too, if he has to."

So, when they set off ten minutes later, there were three of them. Jerry kept racing on ahead, and then running back to rejoin them.

"Just like a hyperactive dog," commented Grandpa. "If I had a bone, I'd throw it to him. Do him good, though, to run off some of that crossness."

When they came to the Container Port, Jerry wanted to read all the labels on the giant boxes — some as big as house trailers — and to guess what was in them. The enormous gantry cranes were in operation, picking up the containers as though they were matchboxes, and loading them onto a waiting ship.

"Ever neat!" breathed Jerry, and it was hard to pull him away for the rest of the walk. Then, when they reached the sea wall, he was almost more excited.

But he didn't say anything. He just stood there, stock-still, and looked at it all. With the sun in the west, the sea was a deep blue, and the bright colors of a passing ship were brilliant against it. Gulls were swooping and screeching above them; and way out beyond them was the open and empty horizon. Finally Jerry was able to speak. "Why didn't someone tell me about all this?" he said. He used the same words that Oliver had used in his head. "This place is *A-okay*."

Later on, as they walked along beside the sea, they came to what looked like a big fort. The boys ran up to it, and climbed on top of it, around it, and inside it. "Hey, Grandpa," yelled Jerry, "what is it?"

"It was a gun emplacement and surveillance station used during earlier wars. From here, the soldiers could see far out to sea, and would know if there were enemy ships or submarines out there."

"C'mon, Grandpa," pleaded Oliver. "Tell us some more about the fort."

"Well," said his grandfather, "it's very, very old. The first part of it was built in 1762 —"

"Seventeen sixty-two!" Jerry couldn't believe it.

"Yes, all that time ago. Then they kept changing it and improving it when something big was going on, like the

American Revolution and the Napoleonic Wars. They had cannon in it, and were ready for anything that might threaten the peace."

"Like what?" asked Oliver.

"Like the French who'd attacked Newfoundland. Or like the Americans, during the War of 1812. After that, they put in some stonework and built those concrete structures in 1888, when they got new quick-fire guns."

"Did they ever have a big battle right here?" asked Jerry.

"No," said Grandpa. "All these fortifications, and they were never really used against an enemy. This apparently war-like city has been a very peaceful place. But then . . ." he paused.

"But then what?" asked Jerry.

"Oh, I don't know," said their grandfather. "It just seems strange. Not a shot fired, and yet one-third of the city was destroyed on one single awful morning in 1917."

"The Explosion," said Oliver.

"Yes," said Mr. Fraser. "The biggest explosion in the world, until the first atom bomb was dropped."

"Wow!" exclaimed Jerry, putting his two fists up to his eyes like binoculars, and pretending to look for submarines. "Now, tell us more about the last big war, Grandpa."

And he did. He told them interesting stories about what Halifax was like during the Second World War, and even way back before that. "I never did get overseas in the last war," he said, "but there were lots of amazing things to see in this city during those days. From where we're standing, we could watch the biggest naval parades of that time setting off for Europe with dozens of ships moving out of the harbor in convoy — to protect each other during the long trip to Europe."

Then, Oliver found something in one of the surveillance balconies. It was a picnic table. "Hey, Grandpa!" he yelled. "Look! Here's something that makes me feel real good."

Grandpa and Jerry looked at it, puzzled. "Why?" said Jerry. "What's so great about that?"

But Oliver didn't answer. Suddenly he felt closed up again. If they couldn't see what was so great about a picnic table sitting in a place that used to be crammed full of guns, he didn't feel much like explaining.

* * *

On Sunday night, Oliver wrote one of his secret letters to his father.

Dear Dad,

Yesterday we went to the Park. It was beautiful down there and the sea was wonderful and very blue. There are all kinds of forts and things around the edge of the water and even in the woods.

The forts were lots of fun to walk around and climb over, but after a while I started to think, Why are there so many wars? It's like almost everyone lives through at least one. Is there something about us human beings that wants war? Is it the same as people wanting to be bullies? And why do they feel like that? What makes a bully be a bully? And how can you stop them without being a bully yourself? These were hard questions, and I didn't know how to answer them.

Then I saw something that made me feel awful. It was a big round many-sided monument on a sort of lawn place, overlooking the sea. It had names all over it of people who'd died in different wars and hadn't even been found or buried. They were lost people. There was one list that was really long. It was for the First World War. It was a list of medical personnel. It was just the people from around here and just the ones who had never been found. The names went on and on, and I counted the ones who had been nurses. I don't want to say how many there were.

Up to now, I was worried about you, but something inside me tried to believe that no one would bomb a hospital. But now I know that's not true. Hospitals can get bombed by mistake. Or perhaps even on purpose. Or maybe nurses and doctors go out on battlefields to rescue people and get shot themselves. Dad, now I'm scared blue. Sometimes I almost wish I didn't love you so much. And I feel like nowhere in the whole world is safe — not even this blue house.

> *Love,*
> *Your son,*
> *Oliver.*

Oliver put this letter in his drawer with the other ones.

Thirteen

O n Monday morning, Harry called for Oliver, and a couple of Jerry's new friends turned up, too. They started off for school in a small parade, cheerful in the bright morning sunshine.

"Does me good," said Grandma to her husband, "to see those boys with new friends. It must be hard for them watching their whole world turn upside down, all at one time. Old friends gone, house gone, school gone, father gone."

"I suppose so," said Grandpa. "But they've got new friends and a new house and a new school now. Doesn't sound so terrible to me. I guess it's hard for them to be missing their father, but my own father was such a cranky pain in the neck that I can't really imagine breaking my heart over him if he'd left home for a while."

"Jerry seems better today," said Grandma. "Not so hepped-up and mad at everything."

"Maybe the Park did it. He seemed to like it. Gave him a way to let off steam — running all over the place and jumping over things. I used to need that when I was a kid. I remember leaving the house when Pa would be in one of his rages, and I'd just run and run for ages. Sometimes I'd run clear up to the top of the Citadel, and then race round and round the moat up there, until I nearly dropped. When I came down, I felt like I could cope a little better."

"That's probably why you walk so much now," said Grandma.

He looked at her in surprise, and brought his brows together, frowning, thinking. Then he said, "You could be right." He chuckled. "Guess I should buy a tread-mill."

Grandma grinned. "The thought," she said, "has oc-curred to me a hundred times."

* * *

When the kids got closer to the school yard, Oliver walked along in silence. This was the day he'd probably get it between the eyes from Gus. Suddenly it didn't matter that the sun was shining. Even a storm might have been kind of satisfying, bending the trees over and matching his mood.

And there was Gus, sitting on the tire swing, moving slowly from side to side and back and forth. He was looking straight ahead of him, face blank. His gang sat on the jungle gym, saying nothing. The equipment was supposed to be for the younger kids, but when Gus was using it, they stayed at the other end of the yard.

"What's up with Gus?" asked Harry but no one could answer him. Then the boys noticed that there were little groups of kids all over the yard, huddled around one another and whispering. Harry walked up to one of them and demanded, "What gives?"

"Didn't you hear?" said one boy. "Gus's father's wounded. That's why he stayed home on Friday. Some-thing wrong with his legs. He was standing right near when a land mine went off. Didn't blow his legs *off*, but

I guess it sure made mincemeat of them. Maybe he'll walk again. Maybe not. My dad told me."

Suddenly Oliver felt sick to his stomach. He realized that he'd been hating Gus really hard and secretly wishing that bad things would happen to him. But not something like *this*. Oliver almost felt as though he'd planted that land mine himself. He felt *guilty*. He knew it was stupid to feel that way, but he couldn't help it.

All through the morning and afternoon classes, Oliver kept sneaking looks at Gus. He looked as though he'd been run over by a truck. All red and swollen around the eyes, messed-up hair, and that awful blank expression on his face. He didn't even pick up a pencil or a book all day long, and none of the teachers bothered him. Even Mr. Hennigar held off on his lecture about the copied assignment.

So, after school got out that day, Oliver waited to see if Gus would go to hockey practice. He didn't. Most of the members of his gang were on the team, so when Gus started off for home, he was all alone. He walked very slowly, with his shoulders hunched over and his feet dragging.

Gus lived way down on the south end of Tower Road. Oliver walked behind him, but they'd almost reached Gus's home before Oliver could make himself speak. Finally, he caught up with him. He was scared to say anything, but he had to.

"Hey, Gus," he said, "don't get mad, but I just wanted to say, I'm, well, sorry about your dad. Getting wounded and all."

Gus turned around and glared at him. "Stupid little jerk!" he growled. "*Your* dad won't get hurt. Sitting around safe, in a nice white hospital."

"He's not safe," snapped Oliver, feeling himself get mad all over again. "And it's not white. It's a bunch of tents. And other stuff holding them together. And he's not sitting around. Hospitals sometimes get bombed. Nurses and doctors get killed. Last night on TV I heard about a nurse and a doctor who got tangled up in a land mine. Americans. *Dead* Americans."

Then Oliver looked hard at Gus. "Lookit," he said. "There's something you gotta see. C'mon. I'll show you." He grabbed Gus's arm.

Gus must have been too dazed to know what he was doing, because he followed Oliver all the way down to Point Pleasant Park. Neither of them spoke as they walked along, and they didn't once stop until they got to the War Memorial monument. Then Oliver stood in front of the long list of medical personnel who'd been killed in one of the old wars. "Look," he said. "Count them. Doctors, nurses. Not just wounded. Dead. And those are just the ones they couldn't find. There must be zillions of others. *Dead*."

Gus stood in front of the list, and looked at it for a long time, without speaking. Then he walked slowly over to the picnic table inside the old fort nearby, and sat down. He put his elbows on the table, and covered his face with his hands.

Oliver sat down beside him and didn't say anything. He didn't look at him, either, because Gus's breathing was kind of funny, and Oliver thought maybe he was crying. He knew that Gus would never forgive anyone who saw that happen.

After a while, Oliver saw out of the corner of his eye that Gus had taken his hands away from his face and was just looking out to sea. It was sheltered in the fort, and the air had the feel of spring in it. The sun beat down on their backs, and Oliver unbuttoned his coat.

Finally, he said, "Is he hurt bad?"

"Yes," said Gus. "Legs smashed to bits."

"But not . . ." Oliver couldn't say it.

"Oh, he's still *got* them," said Gus, "if that's what you mean. But they're no damn use. Not now." He paused. "And maybe never will be." His voice sounded like loose gravel.

Oliver hesitated. "Maybe my dad is looking after him. He's likely too heavy for those girl nurses to move around and lift."

Gus snorted. "If it takes six girls to lift him, that's what he'd want. None of this man-nurse stuff for *him*. He likes the chicks too much for *that*."

Oliver didn't say anything.

Suddenly Gus hit the table with his fist. Savagely, he said, "All the time chasing skirts, my dad, when he was home. That's why my mom left."

"Left! Your mom *left*?"

"Yeah."

"Where'd she go?"

"Dunno. We just woke up one day, and here was this note on the kitchen table. *I can't stand it anymore. Helen.* That's all it said. Not *Love, Mom,* or anything like that. It was like she wasn't speaking to me at all. Just Dad. Never even sent a postcard. Except once, for my birthday in August, two years ago. It was a card with a palm tree on it. It arrived three days late. It said, *I miss you. Happy Birthday. Mom.* Some lot she missed me. You don't just *take off* if you think you're gonna *miss* someone."

"Holy!" breathed Oliver. "Ever awful." He tried to think what it'd be like if his mother just up and left, but he couldn't plug his mind into that idea at all. She just never would do it. He knew it.

Then he asked Gus, "When did your dad leave Halifax?"

Gus frowned. "He didn't leave Halifax. He left Washington."

"Washington!"

"Yeah. He's American. So'm I. My dad left for the Gulf way back in August. The day *before* my birthday. Shipped me up here to live with his brother. Just like an old sack of potatoes."

"Is that okay? Living with your uncle, I mean?"

"Okay? Okay for who? When I arrived at the door with my suitcase, my uncle looked like he was greeting Frankenstein or someone."

Oliver didn't know what to say. Finally, he spoke. "Sometimes my grandfather is real cranky and mad. I think he'd maybe like it a lot if we went home. My grandmother says he doesn't know what to do with himself now that he's retired. So he just watches TV and goes on walks and bosses everyone around. But I think he's getting better. I sort of like him. Not much, but a little. Maybe your dad's brother will get better."

Gus looked at him hard. "Does he beat you?" he asked.

"Beat me? Who? Grandpa? You mean, like *hit* me and stuff?"

"Yeah. Does he?"

"No!"

"Well, Uncle Joseph does. When he gets drunk or if I make him mad. Sometimes I have bruises. I hate him." Then he said, "And I hate my father, too. I hate him for going away to war. And he didn't have to send me up here with his dumb brother. *No*. I *love* him." He put his head in his hands again. "I don't know what I feel," he mumbled. Then he hit the picnic table again. He hit it and hit it, until he had red welts on his hands, and blood started to run down between his fingers.

Oliver watched him and said nothing. Then, when Gus had calmed down a bit, he said to Oliver,

"I copied your assignment."

"I know," said Oliver.

"Tomorrow I'm gonna tell Mr. Hennigar."

"Okay," said Oliver.

"You're not mad?"

"I was," said Oliver. "I wanted to kill you. But not now."

They sat very still for a while, and looked out at the horizon. A gray naval vessel was on its way out of the harbor, and an oil tanker was coming in. The sea was such a dark blue that it was almost navy, and the gulls overhead were screeching at one another.

"C'mon," said Oliver. "Come home with me and we'll bandage up your hand. My mom's out, but Grandma knows all about bandages."

* * *

Later on, Gus and Oliver sat in the kitchen of the blue house, eating chocolate chip cookies. Gus's hand had a bandage on it, and he was looking shy but peaceful. When he left, Grandma gave him a big hug, and said, "I hope your father's better, soon." Then Oliver walked with him as far as the corner.

"Lookit, Oliver," said Gus. "My dad didn't just chase skirts. Sometimes he was real nice to me. We did fun things together, like fishing and playing crib and wrestling. Oliver, listen — I saw people fishing out on the breakwater beside the Container Port. Could we do that sometime?"

"Do what?"

"Go fishing. I got two poles. Or I got one and I could borrow Uncle Joseph's. Could we maybe do that, someday?"

"How about after school tomorrow, if it's not snowing or something?"

"Okay. See ya then. And Oliver . . ."

"Yeah?"

"You think there's a chance your father could be looking after my dad's legs?"

"Sure thing. And I bet he'll have them cured in no time at all. He' strong, but he's awful gentle. He'll try real hard not to hurt him. And if you think my grandmother's smart with a bandage, my dad's a real pro."

"See ya tomorrow."

"Yeah. See ya."

* * *

That night, Oliver only had to write one letter to his father.

Dear Dad,

This is an okay place to live. Once you said you might get transferred to Halifax after the war. I think I'd like that fine. I have two new friends. One is Harry, but I already told you about him. The other is Gus — the terrible bully I wrote about before. If there's a Corporal Rogers in your hospital, with busted-up legs, be extra careful of him. He's Gus's dad. I think Gus has a real neat name, don't you? Mom likes her new job. Jerry's okay. Grandma's real nice. Grandpa seems to be better. Not much, but I think he's working on it. But he's been bossing the whole show for so long that I sure don't expect him to turn into a marshmallow overnight.

Love,
Oliver.

Fourteen

Next day, Gus was late getting to school, and all the kids were in the gym when he arrived. He walked in like a tired old man, as though all the juice and strength had been sucked out of him.

Bet he didn't want to come at all, thought Oliver. Bet he thinks about his dad's legs every minute of the day. What can a soldier do if his legs don't work anymore? And I bet he's scared to tell Mr. Hennigar about the copied project. Oliver hadn't told Gus that Mr. Hennigar already knew, because he figured the teacher might be a little softer on Gus if he confessed.

And that's how it was. Gus walked up to Mr. Hennigar as soon as he got in the room and said just four words: "I copied the assignment." Oliver figured that's all he had energy for. Mr. Hennigar looked at him hard. Finally, he said,

"I know this is a tough time for you, Gus. We all know that. But rules are rules. I'm going to have to give you a zero on that assignment, even though I feel sorry for you right now. I don't have to give you a big sermon about the whole thing. You must know you did a bad thing, or else you wouldn't be confessing. And I admire you for it. It takes a lot of courage to admit something like that."

Then Mr. Hennigar went on, "Floor hockey again today. So — go put your sneakers on and see if you can get yourself a goal. Nothing better for misery than a good shot of exercise."

And he was right. Before long, Gus stopped looking like a sleepwalker and was racing up and down the floor, dribbling, intercepting, yelling. Oliver tried, as always, but he was no better at the game than on the first day he'd played it.

The last period of the day was Art, and Oliver did a picture of the view from the sea wall. It was as clear in his head as a photograph. He put in the little beach, the rocky point, the lighthouse to the east, and the evergreen trees along the shore. The sea was a bright blue, and he drew in two flying seagulls and one on the surface of the water, riding the waves.

Miss Menski looked at the picture, and smiled. "Feeling better, today, eh, Oliver?"

He grinned. "A lot better," he said. He knew that the land war that he'd dreaded for so long had started, but that there seemed to be very few allied casualties so far. The TV warned people not to think it was going to be easy, and said that there might be bad things to come. Still, Oliver felt better. And other things in his life were sure looking up.

At 3:30 p.m., Gus whispered, "I've got the poles in my locker. Hurry! Let's go!"

* * *

Down at the end of the long breakwater by the Container Port, Gus and Oliver stood side by side, casting and recovering, casting and recovering. They stayed that way for a long time, without speaking. Finally Gus got a strike and pulled in a big codfish. Then, as they waited for another bite, Gus spoke.

"Do you write letters to your dad?" he said.

"Yeah. Often. Do you?"

"No. But anyways he never writes to me, neither."

There was another pause, while they reeled in their lines and then let them out again.

"Oliver . . ."

"Yeah?"

"When you write your old man, could you maybe ask him to look around his hospital tent to see if he can find my dad? And maybe do something, well, *special,* for him?"

"I already did," said Oliver. "Mailed it this morning."

Gus stared at him with a surprised look on his face, but Oliver didn't see it because his eyes were fixed on the horizon.

"That's where the ships'll come from, when they bring the people home," he said. "Or perhaps they'll come in planes."

Gus was silent again for quite a while. Finally he said, "Something I didn't tell you."

"What?"

"They're gonna send my dad home as soon as he's well enough to travel in a plane. Maybe in two weeks."

"Hey, wow! Way to go!" Oliver turned to Gus with a wide grin.

But Gus wasn't smiling. His line was dangling in the water, and he was staring at the waves below him.

"I don't want him to come," he mumbled.

"*What*?"

"I'm scared. I'm scared to see those legs of his. I'm scared to see my dad in a wheelchair. He always used to tear around like a speed skater. Never did anything slow. Or quiet. Always on the go. Always playing ball or hockey or something. I don't want to see him like he is now."

"Maybe it's not as bad as you think."

"It is. They told us it'll be *at least* six months before he'll be able to even *try* to stand on those legs. And Oliver . . ."

"Yeah?"

"I remember once when he put his back out of kilter."

"And?"

"He had to stay in bed for a week. Just one week. He nearly went crazy. Cranky as a bear, and mad at everything we said or did. Throwing things. Acting like a tiger in a cage. My mom used to shut herself in the bathroom and cry. I watched her through the keyhole."

"Won't he be in the hospital?"

"Yeah. For a couple of months. Maybe longer. Here, instead of Washington, because there's no one to look after me there. That'll be okay, I guess. But then he'll come home. To Uncle Joseph's."

"Maybe your uncle won't beat you up anymore, if your dad's around."

Gus snorted. "Or beat me up *worse*. This morning he said to me, 'When you came, I had to start running a bloody boarding house. Now it looks like I'm going to be operating a damned hospital. I never *asked* for any of this!' Then he picked up a glass jar of peanut butter and threw it against the wall so hard that it broke. Peanut butter dribbling all down the wall and over the carpet. Oliver . . . ?"

"Yeah?"

"When my dad comes home, can I come over to your house sometimes and maybe sit in the kitchen with your grandmother? Or we could do other things. Maybe you could teach me how to draw. Or I could show you how to play hockey."

"I don't think I can learn, but . . ."

"And I don't think I could ever draw, but we could . . ." He paused.

"Try," said Oliver. "We sure could try."

* * *

That evening, at supper time, it seemed as though Oliver's family was right back where it started when the Kovaks had first arrived. Grandpa scolded Grandma because the soup wasn't hot enough. Said that after thirty-nine years of marriage she should be able to make decent soup. Grandma removed his bowl, her face grim and frozen.

"All he had to say," said Oliver's mother, when she followed Grandma into the kitchen, "was, 'Would you mind heating up my soup, please?' He didn't have to make a federal case out of it. Mom! Why didn't you tell him off?"

Grandma swung around and faced her daughter. "Why don't *you?* " she said sharply. "Go right on in and give it a try. Then settle down to three long days of bleak looks and the silent treatment. Do it! I'm tired of you scolding *me* when *he* gets mad. If you're so much braver than I am, go ahead and tell him off yourself!"

Mrs. Kovak sighed. "You know I can't do that, Mom," she said. "I'm a guest in his house. I can't have big fights with him as long as I'm living here."

"Well," said Grandma, "you're in *my* house now, too. If I'm too big a wimp to stand up to him, I can at least stand up to you."

Mrs. Kovak wilted. She put her arm around her mother's shoulders. "Gee, Mom, I'm sorry. There's so much bad stuff going on. I'm just so worried. The war. Being your kid again instead of a mother and wife. Thinking about what I'll do if anything happens to Sam. And I'm taking it all out on you."

"And your father's taking it out on us because he hates being retired. Jerry's taking it out on the whole world because he's worried about his father and sad about moving here. And Oliver . . ."

Mrs. Kovak smiled. "And Oliver's fine. I don't ever have to think about him."

Grandma scowled at her daughter. "He's not fine, Jill, and it's time you *did* do some thinking about him."

"What?" Mrs. Kovak stared at her mother. "What on earth are you talking about?"

Grandma had picked up the tray of desserts and was already on her way to the dining room. She didn't have time to say much more, but as she walked towards the door, she added,

"I'm talking about how it's time you got to know your own child. I may be a wimp, but there are ways in which I already know him better than you do. Stop expecting him to be such a giant. And pick up that coffee, please, and bring it in with you."

Mrs. Kovak picked up the coffee pot and walked slowly back into the dining room. She sat down and started to pour coffee into the three cups on the table. Turning to Oliver, she asked,

"How are things, Oliver?"

"Fine," he said.

She shot her mother a triumphant look. Then she turned back to him. "*Really* fine, Oliver? Please tell me. I need to know. Are you telling me the truth? It's okay, you know, to admit it if you feel awful."

Oliver looked at her for a moment before he answered. "Pretty good, today, Mom," he said. "A heck of a lot better than last week. Last week was terrible."

"*Terrible*? But last week you said you were fine."

"Well, I wasn't. I felt like I was dying."

"*Why*?" Mrs. Kovak was twisting her napkin into a long snake. "*Tell me*."

"Oh, you know. Rough stuff. A bully was hassling me a lot. And someone stole my assignment. And I was accused of cheating. And Mr. Hennigar treated me like a lazy dumbbell. And the war —"

"Oh, Oliver," said Mrs. Kovak, with her fist pressed against her mouth. "I'm sorry. I didn't know. I guess I was too closed up in my own worries and wanted to believe you were all right. Are things better now?"

"You bet!" grinned Oliver. "The bully's my friend, I got a hundred in my assignment, everyone knows I didn't cheat, and even Mr. Hennigar has stopped bugging me."

Mrs. Kovak sighed with relief. "Then everything's perfectly okay again," she said.

Oliver took a deep breath before he answered. He had to give himself time to think about what he was going to say. He looked over at his grandmother, and she was ever so slightly nodding at him.

"No," he said. "It's not perfectly okay."

Mrs. Kovak looked puzzled. "What else is wrong, then?" she said. "Sounds pretty good to me."

"And to me," growled Grandpa, and his wife shot a frown in his direction.

Jerry was just sitting there, taking it all in, eyes hopeful.

"The war is what's wrong," said Oliver. "Me and Jerry worry a lot about Dad. We don't want to say so because we know you're unhappy, but *we're* scared and sad a lot of the time, too. And all that TV stuff sometimes makes us half crazy with fear."

Oliver stopped talking, full of amazement. Had he actually said all those things? He looked over at his grandmother and grinned. *Ex*-wimps, he thought, and laughed out loud.

Everyone looked at him, startled. Laughter! Now I've done it, he thought. Now no one'll ever figure out who I really am or what I really think or want.

Never mind, thought Oliver, as he dug into his apple pie. Maybe Harry can come fishing tomorrow with Gus and me. The weatherman says it's going to be pretty warm tomorrow, at least for February 27th. Sometimes the winter ends early in Nova Scotia.

Epilogue

T he Gulf War ended on February 27, 1991, the day following the scene in the last chapter of *Oliver's Wars*. Most of the Canadian medical personnel returned home by plane in March of that year. The others came back by ship, sailing into Halifax on the morning of April 7.

There were surprisingly few casualties among the Coalition forces, and not one Canadian serviceman or woman was killed. However, just as Oliver had feared, many thousands of Iraqi servicemen and civilians were either killed or wounded during the war.

The First Canadian Field Hospital looked after Priority One casualties requiring urgent treatment, giving medical care to both Coalition and Iraqi service personnel.

Equipped with surgeons and specially trained nurses and medical assistants, the hospital would have been able to treat a person as severely wounded as Gus's father.